FAULT LINE

FAULT LINE

C. DESIR

Simon Pulse

New York   London   Toronto   Sydney   New Delhi

SIMON PULSE

An imprint of Simon & Schuster Children's Publishing Division

1230 Avenue of the Americas, New York, NY 10020

First Simon Pulse hardcover edition November 2013

SIMON PULSE and colophon are registered trademarks of Simon & Schuster, Inc.

For information about special discounts for bulk purchases, please contact Simon & Schuster Special Sales at 1-866-506-1949 or business@simonandschuster.com.

The Simon & Schuster Speakers Bureau can bring authors to your live event. For more information or to book an event contact the Simon & Schuster Speakers Bureau at 1-866-248-3049 or visit our website at www.simonspeakers.com.

Interior design by Hilary Zarycky

The text of this book was set in New Caledonia.

Manufactured in the United States of America

2 4 6 8 10 9 7 5 3 1

Library of Congress Cataloging-in-Publication Data

Desir, Christa

Fault line / C. Desir. — 1st Simon Pulse hardcover ed.

p. cm.

Summary: After his girlfriend, Ani, is assaulted at a party, Ben must figure out how he can help her to heal, if he can help her at all.

ISBN 978-1-4424-6072-0

[1. Acquaintance rape—Fiction. 2. Rape—Fiction. 3. Dating (Social customs)—Fiction. 4. Emotional problems—Fiction. 5. High schools—Fiction. 6. Schools—Fiction.] I. Title.

PZ7.D4506Fau 2013

[Fic]—dc23

2012039167

ISBN 978-1-4424-6074-4 (eBook)

To those who have shared their stories with me, I am deeply humbled by your courage and deeply grateful for your trust. And to Julio, who loves even the broken pieces of me.

Acknowledgments

This book came out of the Voices and Faces Project Survivor Testimonial Writing Workshop. I am so truly grateful to Anne Ream and R. Clifton Spargo for their guidance and support and for putting so much heart into this work. I wouldn't be here without either of you. Also to all the survivors who have shared their stories with me in that workshop and over the years in hospital ERs or other places, thank you for your trust and for your truth.

I would also not be here without my incredible agent, Sarah LaPolla, who has talked me off more ledges than I can count. Seriously. And without Anica Mrose Rissi for taking a chance on a book that I thought would never be published. And without Liesa Abrams, who poured so much editing love over this book that it sparkled. And without Michael Strother, who wears *all* the hats. Thanks to Jessica Handelman for my gorgeous and fearless cover. I adore you, Team Pulse.

I have so much gratitude for my alpha readers, who read everything I write and tell me they love it: Rebecca (who first asked where the rest was!), Molly, Bergl, Jeannie, Paige, Bruce, and my Desir family. And equal gratitude for those who read what I write and tell me I need to fix it: Carrie, Stephanie, Katy, Amy, Jus, Rebekah, Matt, and Cindy. And to the community of writers and bloggers who have followed me on this journey and have lifted me up in so many ways: *Thank you*. I love my Dark Darlings. You all rock.

The publishing world is pretty small, and I feel like I've had a lot of guardian angels. To Heather Howland and Mandy Hubbard. Thanks. You both read this book when it wasn't ready and told me what I needed to do to get it there. I'm grateful to Vicki, Suzy, JJ, and Helena, who tweet about whiskey, autumn, and darkness and still manage to make me laugh. And to the Fourteenery, who took me in and listened. A lot.

Also, huge love for my teen betas. You are who I write for. I love that you text me or FB message me back within minutes, no matter what time of day it is. I love that you tell me what things are called *now*. I love that you will let me interview you and will read my books even though some of you "don't really read." You remind me every day why I do this.

To awesome writers who have become incredible friends: Jolene, Jay, and Lucy. I couldn't get through a week without any of you. I couldn't get through three days without any of you. I'm glad I talked you into me.

And finally, a mountain of thanks and love to my family.

To my mom, who has watched my kids and played hours of baseball in the backyard with them. To my dad and stepmom, who taught me about the challenges and opportunities that life has to offer. To my sister, who gave me my first YA book and who continues to call me even when I disappear into edits. To my kids, who make me laugh and make me glad that I'm alive every single day. And to Julio, who has always been my center line, my first, my last, my everything. I love you.

FAULT LINE

1

I thought Ani could be fixed. The pieces of her recemented so everything could be how it was. How we were. Until I saw her on her knees in front of Mr. Pinter, his fingers clenched around her ponytail. His face contorted and his head tipped back. He'd been in such a hurry, he hadn't bothered to close all the blinds in his classroom. Or maybe he left the last one open on purpose.

She locked eyes with me as she stood, her hand wiping her mouth, but nothing registered on her face. She tightened the belt on her dark blue winter coat and brushed away the dust it'd picked up from the floor. She smoothed down her collar with steady hands and still held my gaze.

Disgust and anger and so much brokenness swirled together inside me, collecting in the pit of my stomach. I stumbled back a step. This was my Ani. My Ani as she was now.

She blinked twice and finally turned away to grab her faded green backpack from off one of the student desks. A haze of nothingness clung to her.

I stood shaking, my eyes adjusting their focus from the inside of the room to my own reflection in the window. The overlarge hat Ani had knitted me tilted too much to the side. I snatched it off and turned to the bushes behind me. Cold wind sliced across my face, but I didn't feel it like I should have. I took one step and crumpled, as the image of Ani slammed back into my mind. Fingers pawing at the frozen ground, I puked until my stomach had nothing left. Until my insides mirrored Ani's empty face.

I lifted myself on wobbly legs and realized for the first time since I'd met her, I was never going to be able to save my girlfriend.

Six months earlier

It was stupid to hang out in the mostly deserted parking lot of the 7-Eleven. The cops always showed up and sent us away, threatening us with charges of loitering. But Kevin wanted a cherry Slurpee and none of us wanted to get home before curfew. I sat on the bright yellow parking bumper block, tossing pennies at a Dr Pepper bottle I'd set up and listening to the guys argue about where to buy beer without getting carded.

2

The pennies jingled in my hand as I launched another one at the Dr Pepper. *Plink*.

"Nah, man, that chick got fired last week for not carding. We can't go to the KwikMart."

Plink.

"That blows. That girl was a guarantee. Should we try the grocery store, then?"

Plink.

"Hell no, they've got video cameras at that place. And all those frickin' 'We Card Because We Care' posters on the walls. We gotta go somewhere small."

Plink. Saturday nights sucked. The conversations never changed.

A faded blue minivan rattled into the parking slot next to my Dr Pepper setup, and a leggy girl opened the passenger door and slid out. Too-loud zydeco music poured from the van as she leaned in to grab her wallet. Her dark blond hair was pulled into a knot on top of her head. She had on a black clingy tank top and jeans with too many holes in them. I stopped tossing pennies and slowly checked her out. Pink toes in flip-flops, curvy hips, too-skinny waist.

"Your hair makes you look like an asshole," she said as soon as my eyes reached her chest.

Plink. Plink. Plink. Plink. Pennies dropped beside me. I ran my hand through the tight curls of the Mohawk I'd been sporting since the beginning of summer. She followed my movement and smirked.

"Your mouth makes you sound like a bitch," I answered.

"Huh. Decent comeback." She placed her hand on her hip and looked me over like she was assessing a car. I wanted to throw my shoulders back and puff out my chest, but I knew the guys would never let me hear the end of it. So I dropped my hands to my sides and let her look. Her gaze locked on the fly of my jeans.

Whoa. Ballsy girl. I probably would've blushed if the guys weren't watching me. Instead, I dropped my knees open and her gaze quickly shifted to the side. Ha. Thought so.

"Do you live here?" Her focus returned to my face.

"At the 7-Eleven?" I asked.

She turned to the guys, who'd obviously forgotten their beer-finding mission to watch me fumble through a conversation with the hot girl none of us had ever seen before.

They shook their heads and grinned at me. Ass munches. They loved to give me shit when it came to the opposite sex.

"Do you live here?" she asked me again.

"Yeah," I finally answered.

"Well, now so do I. I'm Annika," she said, and grabbed a hoodie out of the open door of the van.

I didn't stand up. I should have, but that sort of thing would've sent a definite message to the guys and I wasn't up for spending the rest of my night getting crap from them.

"Ben . . . but most of my friends call me Beez."

She tapped her finger against her lips and looked me up and down again. "Of course they do. I'll see you around . . . Ben."

She slipped her hoodie on and sauntered into the 7-Eleven like she had no idea five guys were checking out her ass. She looked back when she opened the door and gave me a little wink.

"Beezus," Kevin said, smacking me on the shoulder, "looks like you've found yourself a little hottie."

I gathered up my pennies and tried to hide the red on my cheeks. Kevin dropped to the space on the parking bumper next to me.

Plink.

"I don't know about that. I don't normally go for girls who call me an asshole the first time I meet them."

Kevin laughed and snatched one of the pennies from me. "Dude, you totally do."

Plink.

2

"You're gonna be late. Banana bread French toast is downstairs waiting for you," my mom called from the bottom of the stairs. The high ceilings in our front hallway made her voice echo and I winced again at the bigness of our house. We'd "relocated" to the nicer part of town after my dad got some major work promotion. Our old house was fine, but painting and redecorating projects made Mom happy.

"Banana bread French toast? Seriously? I can't believe you're still doing this. It was cute when we were five. It's sort of ridiculous now," I answered, making my way past our wall of family photos and down the stairs two at a time. My feet barely touched each hardwood step before I hopped to the next one. I *may* have been a little psyched about the possibility of seeing Annika again. Eight days of hopeful drives through town and made-up errands to the 7-Eleven had me frustrated and wound up.

Mom squeezed my cheek when I reached her and I ducked out of the way. She reached out to pat the top of my head, her only acknowledgment of the twenty minutes I'd spent in the bathroom with a razor.

"Thanks for indulging me. This will be your last year, you know." She gave me the weepy mom eyes and I snorted.

My brother, Michael, was already sitting at the table, leafing through a gamer magazine. His curly hair was uncombed and he had toothpaste on his shirt. I flicked his ear.

"I'll give you a ride to school, shrimp, but you're on your own afterward. I've got to grab some food before swim club."

"S'okay," my brother mumbled. "I've got youth orchestra anyways."

I eyed the black case at Michael's feet. It sort of sucked he wasn't good at any sports. I worried how he was going to manage next year. It's not a big deal playing clarinet in the fifth grade, but that shit'll get you crucified in junior high. A large faded book of *Classics for the Clarinet* stuck out of his unzipped backpack.

Michael followed my eyes to the book. He shrugged. "I'm competing for first chair."

"How many people are you going up against?"

Michael grinned. "Two, but I'm pretty sure I'll get it."

I nodded and dropped into the chair next to him. Michael was a really good musician. Part of me hoped he'd stick with it in spite of the beating he'd likely take for it.

"I can pick you up after school, sweetie," Mom said, ruffling Michael's hair. He didn't flinch. I gave my mom maybe two more years of hair ruffling before he started to duck away from her too.

She turned toward the counter and started to dish food onto a plate.

"So, Ben, are you excited about your senior year?" She placed a giant stack of French toast in front of me.

"Mom. Really? We're not going to have this conversation, are we?" I poured half the bottle of syrup on my French toast and forked it into quarters.

"Oh, come on," she said, setting a large glass of milk next to me. "Humor me. What's your main goal for the year?"

A quick image of Annika's long legs flashed in my mind. I grinned but kept my thoughts to myself. Mom probably wouldn't appreciate me sharing *that* goal. I took a large bite, barely chewing before swallowing the lump of gooey sweetness. Banana bread French toast. The most brilliant food blending since chocolate-covered pretzels.

I gulped down half the glass of milk, then answered, "My main goal? Scholarship, Mom. You know that. I want to swim for Iowa."

"Don't worry, you'll get it," my brother said through a mouthful of French toast. He made a strange humming noise when he ate. I shook my head. This kid was never going to get a girlfriend.

"Thanks for the vote of confidence, shrimp." I glanced at the clock. "Now, hurry up, we need to roll so we're not late. I hate finding parking on the first day of school."

I wolfed down the rest of my breakfast in two bites and stuck my tongue out to lick the plate. Mom snatched it away before I could clean it off completely.

"Home on time, Ben," she said, pointing to my face, then the napkin next to me. "Your dad wants to do a celebratory first-day-of-school dinner at the Marion Street Grill."

"Oh, Jesus, he's leaving work early?" I glanced at the napkin and then rubbed syrup off my chin with my sleeve.

"Yes." Mom squinted. In a quick move, she grabbed the napkin and dipped it in Michael's water, dabbing at the sides of my mouth. I pushed her hand away and stood up.

"You guys need to stop reading all those parenting books. All this 'quality time' isn't good for us. It's giving us a very distorted view of the 'average American family' and you know we'll just have unrealistic expectations about our future wives and ultimately end up as divorced alcoholics who spend thousands of dollars in therapy because our parents created an 'unattainable ideal,'" I said, employing mom air quotes as much as I could. Michael snorted. The two of us were merciless with air quotes, but Mom still wouldn't give them up.

She also constantly played "how to raise healthy kids and maintain your relationship" type audiobooks in her car. I'd forgotten my iPod enough to be able to recite most of them by heart.

"Ben," Mom answered in a chipper voice, "that's more words than you've said to us in two months. I'm delighted to see our 'nefarious plan' to include you in this family is working. We'll see you at the Marion Street Grill at six." She kissed my head and handed me my backpack.

The first day of school reeked of the same bullshit every year. All the teachers gave mind-numbing lectures about class expectations and the importance of turning in assignments on time, while we stared out the windows at the too-green lawn and too-blue sky, wishing summer break lasted a few more weeks. The halls filled with squealing girls talking about their vacations as if they hadn't texted each other every day. New clothes, new hair, new couples. Same crap.

I wandered between classes, searching the freshly painted halls for Annika. Sucky scenarios where she was homeschooled or went to Catholic school kept popping into my head, but I pushed them back. I was a senior. This was the Year of Beez. Kevin met me at the door of the cafeteria, his stocky frame bouncing from foot to foot. He wasn't built to swim, but he could hold his breath longer than any guy on the team. He started in on me as soon as we found a table, before I could even put ketchup on my fries.

"Dude, have you seen Annika?"

"No." I took a bite of fry. "Have you?" *Please. Please. Please.*

"No, but I heard some of the swim guys talking about her. Fresh meat and all."

Anger and relief battled in my gut. She was *here.* But dammit, the guys already knew about her. I cringed. I didn't want to get all possessive since she wasn't really mine, but it bugged the crap out of me that other people were interested in her. Maybe thinking about her legs too.

Kevin must have seen the irritation on my face. "Don't worry, dude. I told them you'd already staked your claim."

"I haven't staked my claim. I'm not a caveman." I'd totally staked a claim, but I wasn't about to tell Kevin.

"Whatever you say, man. Hey, did you hear Morgan's having a back-to-school party this weekend?"

I grunted in response. Morgan's house was awesome, full game room in the basement, five bedrooms upstairs, parents who spent weekends at their place in Michigan, but she was more trouble than she was worth. Always had been.

"Come on, man. It's not like you have to hang out with her. There're gonna be, like, a thousand people there. Five kegs and Jack's band is playing." Kevin was ADD and could be like a hyper puppy when he had his mind set on something. If I didn't shut him down, he'd mention Morgan's party fifteen more times before lunch ended.

"I'll think about it."

Kevin smiled. "Probably Annika'll be there."

I grinned back. He was totally playing me, but it didn't matter. We'd been friends forever and he knew how to push my buttons as much as I did his.

"I said I'd think about it."

He punched my arm. "You'll be there. I know you, dude, and you won't be able to resist."

The afternoon dragged on and even though I kept hoping I'd see Annika, she didn't end up having any classes with me. Probably she was in all those AP classes with the poseurs who pretended they didn't care about grades, but then did shit like take classes at the community college on the weekend and over the summer.

The parking lot was a bitch to get out of after school. I usually waited fifteen minutes for everything to clear out before I ventured to my car, and even then the lot wasn't always empty. People leaned on hoods, playing music out open windows, wanting to be seen with the cars they'd nagged their parents to buy them when they turned sixteen. Not that I could really talk, since Dad had handed over a set of keys on my last birthday, but at least his reason for doing it involved carting Michael around. And being the designated driver for my friends.

Kevin was riding shotgun in my POS Jeep and going on about whether some junior girl I barely knew had gotten a boob job over the summer when I finally saw Annika. She had on shorts and a scoop-neck black shirt that showed off the bones of her neck. She leaned over to unzip a backpack that rested at her feet and I followed the line of her bare legs, which were even better than I imagined. I rolled my window down.

"Annika!" I called. She looked up and a small smile tugged at her lips.

"Where's your Mohawk, Bumble?"

I scrubbed my hand over my newly shaven head. "Apparently, it makes me look like an asshole. And it's Beez."

"Oh, of course, that's right. Well, I hope you didn't shave it on my account," she said, but I thought I saw a spark of interest in her eyes. Hoped it was a spark of interest. I switched off the car radio and hung my elbow out the window.

"Don't flatter yourself. I'm a swimmer." I didn't mention that last year I sported the Mohawk for most of the swim season and didn't go completely bald until regionals.

"Huh. I thought swimming was more of a white guy sport?"

"Whoa. Did you just say that . . . out loud?"

She tilted her head. "Yeah. Feel free to tell me I'm wrong, but I've seen the team pictures in the gym. And I've watched a lot of college sports. It's pretty white."

"Well," I said, trying to keep my eyes from zeroing in on her tan legs, "I'm half-white and I play basketball sometimes on the weekends so I don't think I'm going to lose my NAACP card."

"I don't know. They're kinda strict about that sort of stuff," she said, and tucked a piece of hair behind her ear.

"Did you come from the South? 'Cause that racist shit doesn't really fly up here."

She flashed me a smile and leaned over to root in her backpack for something. I shifted higher in my seat to peek down her shirt, but she put her hand over the scooped neck and blocked my view.

"No," she said, and pulled out a pair of sunglasses. "I earned the right to make sweeping generalizations about black people after dating the varsity center at my old school. He was six nine. And vain as hell. I practically had to beat down the entire cheerleading squad to get to him after a game. It was no small feat, believe me."

Kevin elbowed me and snorted. "Holy shit, I like this girl."

"Yeah," I called to her, "I'm not sure you'll be able to play that card here. Sweeping generalizations don't really go over too well. You're gonna have to start from ground zero. Most people are just gonna see you as a mouthy white girl." I grinned and stared as her tongue licked her bottom lip. Crap. Did all girls know that move?

She put the sunglasses on her head to hold her hair back.

"Well, I'll let you know if I'm interested in reinitiation. In the meantime, looks like you're backing up traffic. You better run along."

I looked into my rearview mirror and saw a silver Audi idling behind me. A girl was leaning into the driver's-side window, arms stacked beneath her boobs, probably trying to call attention to her cleavage. My guess: The driver wasn't in that big of a hurry.

"Where's your new house?" I asked. Weak and obvious stalling, but I didn't want Annika to walk away yet.

"On Harrison, above Studio Pink."

"Across from Buzz Café? I know that place. Where'd you move from?" I asked. My eyes shifted to check the car behind me; the leaning girl now had her tongue in the driver's mouth. Yeah, I had some time.

"California. Listen, I'd love to play twenty questions with you. Really. But I've got someplace to be." Her eyes darted to the blue minivan that had pulled into the opposite side of the school lot. She slung the backpack onto her shoulder.

"Is that your mom?" I asked.

"That's good deductive reasoning, Ben. I'm glad the removal of all your body hair hasn't affected your brain cell count."

Kevin smacked my arm and chuckled. "This girl's gonna be a pain in your ass."

I shoved him and turned back to her. "Well, I didn't actually shave my whole body, but if you're volunteering your services . . ."

"Pass," she said, and took a step toward her mom's car before swiveling back to me. "But if you want, I'll be home later. My standards are pretty high, but I'm willing to give you a shot." Then she walked the rest of the way to her mom's van without once looking back at us.

It took me a second to absorb what she'd said, but then I looked at Kevin with a huge grin on my face.

"Straight shooter," I said, and flipped the radio back on. "Nice."

"Yep," Kevin agreed. "That's your kind of chick. Although, if she's not feeling you, let me know. I might go for her."

"I don't think so. She's got way too much personality for you, my friend. And I'd venture to guess her boobs are real."

Kevin laughed. "You'll have to let me know later."

I shifted the Jeep into drive and wore a goofy smile all the way to the KwikMart.

A woman with crazy curly hair opened the door when I got to Annika's after swim practice that day.

She crossed her arms and looked me up and down with a small scowl on her face. I blushed and shifted from one foot to the other. Meeting parents sucks.

"You must be Ben?"

I nodded my head. "Nice to meet you. Is Annika here?"

She signaled me inside and directed me to sit on a bright purple couch that smelled a little like bubble bath. The walls were painted orange and there were giant pillows in all colors thrown around the room. I'd apparently walked inside a bag of Skittles.

"You guys unpacked pretty fast, Mrs. . . . um?"

"Yeah, I hate boxes. And you can call me Ms. Taylor, although I prefer to be called Gayle so I'm not constantly reminded of my ex-husband. Do you go to school with Ani or did she pick up a stray at the 7-Eleven?"

I opened my mouth to say something but was interrupted by a girlie laugh. Annika stood in the doorway; light from the living room windows haloed her, and my breath stopped for a second.

"Mom, I don't pick up strays. I checked him out. He's clean. He swims. His dad works in advertising and his mom is a librarian."

"Really?" Her mom looked at me.

I redirected my attention back to Gayle and nodded. I tapped my feet and slumped into the couch. Tiny beads of sweat formed on my bald head. I hated when so much attention was directed at me. But I was psyched Annika checked me out. Did she ask Kevin?

"Yeah, and he's up for some big swim scholarship at Iowa," Annika said, and gave me a wink.

"Good for you, Ben. Best of luck," Gayle said, and her shoulders lowered a fraction.

What the heck kind of parental small talk was this? It sort of felt like I was on a reality TV dating show and my stats were flashing beneath me. The whole thing might've bothered me, but I was too distracted by the way Annika's hair fell in two braids that rested right above the black bra showing through her white shirt. Black bra. Yeah.

Gayle must have suddenly noticed too. She shook her head. "Is that my shirt?"

Annika shrugged. "Maybe. It was in my laundry pile."

"You know it's mine. And you're supposed to wear a camisole underneath it, not a black bra."

The right side of Annika's mouth tilted up. "Huh. Really?"

"Subtle, Ani. You've got two minutes to put a sweatshirt on or change into a different shirt. Jesus. Don't make me play the overprotective mother."

I stared at the ceiling. Every part of my face felt like it was on fire. Were these two seriously having this conversation in front of me? My mom would go ape shit if she were in the room.

I rubbed my hands on my knees and tried to figure out a way to diffuse the awkwardness. "Ani. Cute nickname."

"Yeah, unfortunately Beez was already taken as an option

so I had to go with the far less clever shortening of my given name."

"Ani," Gayle said, and pointed to the door, "the shirt. Now."

Ani smiled at the two of us and shrugged. I gaped at both of them. Weirdest mother-daughter relationship I'd ever seen. Ani adjusted her braids and stuck her tongue out at us. She flounced out of the room.

Gayle pursed her lips. "Sorry. She's trying to get a rise out of me. Both of us, I guess. It's not very often she likes someone enough to invite them over."

I bit back a grin. So this was what zero to sixty felt like. I'd been right about Ani being direct. And she liked me. I let out a breath of relief. She liked *me*. Thank Christ for that. I wasn't really interested in hooking up with a girl who was looking for a bunch of riders on her own train.

"You like her too?" Gayle asked.

"Yeah, I mean we just met, but she's different."

Gayle laughed. "Yes. And special. And very honest. You're lucky. Don't mess it up."

How was I supposed to respond to that? I nodded and directed my gaze to the painting on the wall behind her. It had a bright blue background and showed a thin girl in front with her mouth open and tears in her eyes. From behind, half a dozen orange, green, and purple arms hugged her.

"Did you make that?"

"No. Ani did after her dad left. She's a pretty talented artist."

Ani walked back into the room and my eyes went right to her chest. New shirt. Black, like the bra I no longer could see. Damn. She pulled on a hoodie and zipped it all the way to her chin then pulled the hood strings so we could barely see her face. She looked like one of those Teletubbies.

"Better?" she asked her mom.

"Better," Gayle said. "But you two aren't going into your bedroom. Come on. Let's make Ben something to eat."

Gayle walked out of the room and Ani came to the couch and pulled me up. She unzipped the hoodie and threw it to the side. She leaned toward me and for one heart-stopping second I thought she might kiss me but instead, she sniffed.

"Chlorine?"

"Yeah, I was in the pool before I came over."

"Obviously. Next time, take a longer shower. Or put some lotion on. You're too chemically to kiss."

My head spun. *Kiss*. She'd asked someone about me. And invited me over. And *liked* me. And was maybe going to kiss me. And . . . whoa.

She took my hand and dragged me into the kitchen, where her mom was cutting up fruit and dropping it into a blender. Annika flopped onto a stool and licked her lips. The lips that almost kissed me. My mouth went dry. Crap. This girl was going to chew me up and spit me out.

Her mom left after the smoothies were made and I shifted too much in my seat.

"So swim team, huh?" Ani asked.

"Yeah. Well, it's club right now. Official swim team doesn't start until November, but if you want to stay competitive, you do club."

"Huh. Sounds like you have everything worked out for you."

I shrugged. "I guess. And you paint?"

"Yep. Ever since Mom started carting me around to her classes when she couldn't find a babysitter. Sometimes I make jewelry too." She fingered the pendant on her necklace. "This one's mine."

I leaned forward and tried to keep my eyes on the pendant and not on the way her shirt cut across her collarbone and bunched out in front. "It looks like a tree."

"Yeah. It's a tree of life. It's sort of this symbol to remind me how we're all connected. How something that one person does can change the outcome for so many people. For good or for bad."

"That's deep."

She snorted. "Sorry. You've been in the pool. I don't mean to tax your brain after all that exercise."

"Don't be a smart-ass. I'm not an idiot. I even pass my classes on occasion."

She patted my head. "Of course you do. Don't get huffy."

Her hand slid down to the counter between us. I wanted to take it in mine, I wanted her to touch me again, but I choked. This wasn't how to get a girlfriend. I was supposed to flirt or compliment her or something. But she didn't seem to be looking for any of that.

The space between us became comfortably silent. She scraped her stool next to mine so her knees were pressed into my thigh.

"Tree of life, huh?" I said, leaning closer to her. Not too much but enough.

"Yep." She nudged me with her shoulder. "Everyone's connected."

3

Although I'd promised myself never to deal with Morgan again, like a wuss I picked Kevin up and headed to her party on Friday night. I hadn't asked Ani if she was going to be there, but I figured she'd show if most of the school knew about it.

"You smell kind of good," Kevin said as he hopped into my Jeep. "Big plans for the night?"

I shrugged.

"Are you meeting Ani?" Kevin continued.

"We didn't set up anything specific."

"Probably should have, dude. You know the vultures are gonna swarm once they get a load of those legs."

I whacked him on the shoulder.

"Just saying," he muttered, and shoved me back.

Morgan's street was full of cars, and I guessed we had

maybe a half hour before someone called the cops. The front door to her house was open and the living room was packed with people dancing to music pouring through mounted speakers. So the rumor about Jack's band playing was a lie. Figured. All the furniture was pushed against the peach-colored walls, and through the sliding glass door in the back I could see a bunch of guys outside doing beer bongs. I made a beeline for the keg in the kitchen as soon as we walked in, but Morgan must have been looking out for me, because she blocked my path and wrapped her arms around me the second I entered the room.

"Beezus," she slurred, and raked her fingernails over my head. I shook her off and wiped away her claw marks on my scalp.

"Hey, Morgan."

"I was hoping you'd come." She looked at me with slightly drunk and embarrassingly needy eyes. The kitchen was flooded with too much light, showing exactly how much makeup Morgan had caked on before the party.

"Yeah, I'm meeting someone." Not exactly true, but I hoped it would cut off any further attention from her.

"Really? Who?"

Crap. I hated this, had been dreading it for too long. "Look, Morgan, did you need something?"

She blinked and twisted her long brown hair in her fingers.

"I thought maybe we could talk. You know?" She looked at me hopefully. "About us."

I rubbed my hand over my head. I should have known I wasn't going to get out of this conversation if I showed up at her party. Stupid-ass Kevin and his promises of a thousand people. Damn good thing I'd practiced my speech in the shower.

"Morgan. Listen. You and I don't really work together. I mean, you're nice and all, but we aren't really a good fit." For the love of God, let that be enough.

She opened her mouth, but then peered over my shoulder. I turned around to see that Ani was standing a few feet behind me with a smirk on her face and her arms crossed. Her legs seemed even longer in short cutoffs. And her face was beautiful and fresh, even in the shitty fluorescent lights. I turned back to Morgan.

"I gotta go," I said, and moved away before she could say anything else.

I steered Ani out of the kitchen and pointed toward the front door. She waved me ahead and followed me out of the house. Voices and music from the party carried through the open windows.

"Leaving a trail of broken hearts behind you?" she asked as soon as the door was shut and we'd stepped onto the front sidewalk.

"Oh, Christ, don't you start on me. Girls can be so dramatic."

Ani howled. "Oh, Beez, that's priceless. That poor girl just wants you to talk to her."

"She's an ex who screwed around with one of the other guys on the swim team when I was dating her. She was drunk, but still."

Ani nodded and sat down on the edge of the sidewalk, patting the spot on her right. "Aha. Tricky. Maybe she's trying to make amends?"

I slid next to her and put my elbows on my knees. "Maybe. Probably. It's a little late, though. It wasn't exactly the smoothest breakup."

"Smooth breakups? Have you had many of those?"

"No. Actually, Morgan was the first girl I ever dated." Only girl, until Ani, who I wasn't dating. Maybe.

She slid her hands behind her and leaned back. "She broke your heart?"

"Nah. I mean, I might have said that last year, but really, it was a stupid first crush."

"First girlfriend. Hmm . . . I'm surprised. Not that I had you pegged as a player, but you're kind of the whole package. It's weird no one would've grabbed you by now." I was sort of getting used to the strange honesty of Ani's conversations but still didn't have the first clue what I was supposed to say back.

"Uh . . . thanks?"

"You're welcome." Ani shifted forward. "So how come you came to her party?"

My face flushed and I looked out into the darkness.

Ani elbowed me. "You were hoping I'd show up, weren't you? That's sort of sweet."

"Thanks," I mumbled.

"So let's take a walk," she said, and pulled me up from the sidewalk. "The cops'll be here soon anyways, so we might as well hit the streets."

"Hit the streets? Is that Cali gang talk?"

"Hardly. We lived in a suburb of San Diego. Not exactly gangbanger territory."

We walked slowly toward the corner. I wanted to take her hand but was too nervous to try it. Sort of stupid considering she talked about kissing me the first day of school, but I didn't want to screw things up. She bumped into me three times before I realized she was doing it on purpose and finally got up the nerve to grab her hand.

We wandered through the blocks of McMansions surrounding Morgan's house, talking about school and California and how different things were. Ani told stories about her old friends and laughed in a way I'd never heard a girl do, sort of unself-consciously.

"So my new art teacher said I could use the studio after school if I wanted," she said as she led us back toward Morgan's house.

"That's cool. Have you met a lot of arty people?"

"Some."

"Yeah? Have you met other people?"

"Sure. Why?"

I shrugged. "Just curious."

"Oh, Beez, are you worried I'm not making friends?" she teased.

"No. You probably have a hundred friends already and it's only the first week of school. You're sort of contagious."

Ani barked out a laugh. "Contagious? Gross. Do you mean infectious?"

I turned red. I fricking hated when I didn't get words right and looked stupid. "Yeah. Infectious."

She squeezed my hand, and the warmth of her made me feel like less of an idiot. She was so completely disarming, like all of the usual stupid crap about liking a girl didn't apply with her.

"Well, I don't know about being infectious. But I've met a lot of nice people."

"Like art people?"

Ani raised her eyebrows at me. "Why do you care what kind of people I'm friends with?"

I shrugged. "I don't care. It's just, those art types are kind of elitist."

"Oh. So you're worried what they'll think of you? What they'll say about us?"

I looked down. I didn't care what they thought of me, but I

cared if it threatened the possibility of Ani and me. And I really liked the idea of *us*.

Ani tugged on my ear and I met her eyes. "I don't care what they think. I make my own decisions about people."

I let out the breath I'd been holding. What the hell was my problem? No girl had ever affected me as quickly as Ani did. Of course, no girl I'd ever known was anything like her.

She laughed and pulled me back toward Morgan's front door. I could hear a bunch of people chanting Kevin's name and shook my head at the certainty he was on his second or third beer bong.

"So," I said, stuffing my hands into my pockets.

Ani bit her lip and smiled. I wanted to kiss her, but something stopped me. It didn't feel right standing in front of Morgan's house, knowing I'd have to peel Kevin off the floor in an hour and pray he didn't puke in my car on the way home.

"Now would be the time you ask me on a date," Ani prompted. God, this girl ruled.

"Would you like to go on a date tomorrow night?" I asked.

"Yes, Ben, I would very much like to go on a date with you." She smiled and opened the door into the shouting and cheering of the party. I looked up at the starry sky and closed my eyes as a rush of adrenaline poured over me.

4

I spent an embarrassing amount of time getting ready for my first official date with Ani. I shaved my head and sat on the toilet for forty-five minutes so I wouldn't be caught off guard when I was with her. Michael banged on the door and told me I was stinking up the whole hallway.

"He has a nervous stomach," Mom chided him.

"You both need to go away," I yelled through the door. "What kind of family hovers outside the bathroom when a guy is taking a dump?"

Michael laughed and I heard Mom hissing at him.

My dad was sitting on the sectional couch working on his laptop when I finally came downstairs. His shirt was rolled at the sleeves and he'd slipped his shoes off and stretched his feet on the coffee table. His shoulders slumped as he typed.

He looked fifty years older since he started his new job. His hair had more gray than black. I thought about suggesting he go bald, but decided against it. I didn't want feedback from my parents about how I looked, the least I could do was keep my mouth shut about their aging.

Dad turned to me when he heard the squeak of my shoes on the hardwood floor. His eyes widened and he sniffed.

"Took you a while to get ready."

"First date," I answered.

"The new girl you told us about?" He scanned my jeans critically. My dad didn't leave the house without dress pants on. But showing up in khakis on a first date was for amateurs. Ani would see right through it. In the end, I'd decided the best course of action was to go with jeans, but I threw a collared shirt on for balance.

"Yeah. The girl from school." I grabbed my keys from one of the hooks by the door. Mom's anal organization of the house reached deep.

"The one who makes jewelry?"

I nodded. Date conversations were awkward and I tried to keep my information to my parents to a minimum while still making them think I was sharing things about my life.

"Where'd you say she was from?" he asked, shutting his laptop and placing it on the coffee table.

"California."

"And her mom teaches art?"

"Yeah."

He looked me over again. I could tell he was holding back a dad lecture. I stared up at the front hall light and jiggled my keys in my hand. Dad smoothed the shirt bunched over his stomach. I counted in my head and waited.

My parents would probably spend most of the night speculating about what I was doing. And when I got home Michael would bust into my room and recap the entire humiliating conversation. Dad glanced at his watch and finally nodded.

"You look good. I'm sure you'll sweep her off her feet."

"Thanks," I mumbled, and moved toward the door.

"Honey," Mom called to my dad from the kitchen, "your sister's on the phone."

My dad released a sigh and stood up.

"Everything okay?" I asked.

"Yeah. I think so. Tati Marie's having a hard time right now." The wrinkles on my dad's face looked more obvious as he moved into the hall light.

"Again?" I loved my aunt, but she was a mess and always popping in and out of our lives. I hated how it left my dad depleted.

"She lost her job and needs some help finding a new one."

I didn't say anything.

"I have the resources and she's family, Ben."

I nodded and placed my hand on the doorknob. "Okay. Tell her I say hi."

"Ben," my dad called before walking to the kitchen phone, "don't drink. And be home by curfew. I'll be up, so come talk to me when you get back."

"Sure." I opened the door.

"And you may want to grab some of those wet wipes before you pick her up. The cologne's a little heavy." He chuckled and walked away.

I sighed, shut the door, and headed back upstairs for the packet of wipes. I considered starting over with a new shower, but it was too chicky and I'd already stressed about the date enough.

Ani stood outside Studio Pink waiting for me when I pulled up. The three-story brick building had large gallery windows full of colorful wire sculptures. I'd been inside a few times when I was younger and my family did the holiday art walk, but it'd been years.

"Anxious?" I asked, circling the Jeep to open the door for her.

"Hardly," she answered as she slipped inside the car. "Just tired of all my mom's pesky questions. You'd think it was her date. She kept making all these suggestions about makeup and wardrobe. I couldn't stand it anymore."

I stood at the open door and looked her over. Jeans and a T-shirt, no makeup.

"So . . . I guess you decided not to take her advice," I said.

"Hell no. I'm not that kind of girl. What would be the point of making you think otherwise?"

No games. This girl should be cloned.

"I like your collared shirt, though," she continued. "It shows you care enough to look nice, but your jeans say you aren't so presumptuous that you assume you'll be getting some play later. Nicely done."

I opened and shut my mouth. Ani made me dizzy, like I'd been on a Tilt-A-Whirl too many times at a carnival. I circled to my side of the car and got in.

"I thought we'd see a movie," I said, starting the Jeep.

"No. That's a total first-date cop-out. I can't have a conversation with you if we're watching a movie."

"Okay. Do you have a better idea?" I asked. I wasn't that interested in seeing a movie either, but almost every first date anyone at school went on was at the Lake Street Theater.

"Zoo," she said.

"The zoo? For real? Isn't that for little kids and tourists?"

"You're so judgmental. You have no idea how awesome the zoo is for people watching. And I haven't been to the one out here yet," she said, adjusting the seat belt across her shoulder. I tried not to glance at the T-shirt stretched over her chest, but it was practically impossible.

She shifted toward me. "Can you wait until we're at the zoo to ogle me? It'd be sort of embarrassing to explain to the police we got in an accident because you were checking out my boobs."

My head whipped to the front and she patted my thigh like I was a little kid she'd just reprimanded. Suck.

We parked near the front in the zoo visitor lot and Ani took my hand before I could even stress about the whole hand-holding thing. We passed a bunch of crap souvenir shops, a ten-dollar photo booth, and a carousel of cheesy painted animals, but Ani didn't stop. The paved zoo pathway was sticky with spilled drinks and Canada goose poop, but I powered through, avoiding the obvious droppings.

Ani tugged me toward the elephants and then proceeded to bore me with inane facts about pachyderms. I barely registered what she was saying. I was too busy trying to breathe through my mouth to avoid the smell and worrying that my palms were sweating too much.

She walked us toward a giant building with a sign that said "The Swamp" in painted red letters. I slowed my steps.

"What's wrong?" Ani asked, dropping my hand.

"You want to go inside there?" I pointed to the fake wooden door and the half a dozen baby strollers parked next to it.

"Definitely. Best part of the zoo. The alligator only has one eye. I read it on the website." She nudged me.

"Yeah, maybe I'll just wait here for you." I leaned against the rail beside the strollers.

"Come with me." She tucked her hair behind her ears and batted her eyes at me.

"Ani, I'm not that interested in smelling like ass at the end of the night, and going into any of these buildings is sort of a surefire way."

Ani laughed. "You are adorable. Now let's go. I promise it won't decrease your chances of an end-of-the-date kiss."

I hesitated again, but Ani pushed me inside and made me watch river otters while she enthusiastically extolled the virtues of animal play. And it was sort of cute and playful at first, but then two of the otters started getting pretty frisky, which led to a whole new level of awkward. Ani snorted through the entire thing and I had to practically carry her outside.

"Can we get something to eat?" I asked when we finally exited the building.

"Shit, sorry. I'm sort of making this date suck, aren't I? The otter thing was a bit much, huh?" she asked. Her face opened like she was genuinely curious. She seemed to be looking for some kind of feedback on her dating skills. Crap, it was a classic girl test.

"No, it's fine." Only an idiot would fall for the "be honest with me, am I boring you?" line. Girls never really want to hear an honest answer to *that* question.

"Don't lie to me, Ben. You don't have to bullshit. I can sometimes go overboard with my enthusiasm for animals." She took my hand again and led me toward the food area.

"It's okay. It's sort of cute." And it was, but only because it was Ani. "Do you have any pets?"

She shook her head. "I'm allergic and my mom's a little flaky about things like remembering to feed fish. Pets don't really work with our lifestyle. You?"

"No. They don't really work with our lifestyle either. Plus, my dad always says that animals should be free to roam, not cooped up in a house. His grandparents in Haiti have chickens, but he said they're for eating or selling."

"That's right, I heard you were half Haitian. Have you ever been?" she asked, hopping onto a picnic bench.

"To Haiti?"

She nodded.

"Yeah, a few times. My dad went every summer when he was a kid. But then things got kind of unsafe travelwise so he stopped going when he was sixteen. I'm not exactly sure what happened. I think one of his cousins was mugged at the airport or something. He and my mom went back again after I was born. I haven't been since I was fourteen. It's kind of hard with my mom's grad school schedule and swimming."

I ordered us hot dogs, a hot pretzel, and two Cokes. We sat at the end of the only remotely clean picnic table of the dozen in the food area. Ani ate most of the food. When we finished, she dabbed the mustard off her lips and leaned across the table.

Her kiss startled me and I almost pulled back, but she grabbed the back of my head and tugged me closer. She tasted delicious and kind of gross at the same time.

"What was that for?" I asked, taking a sip of my Coke to wash away her mustard taste.

"I wanted to get it out of the way so you didn't get all weird at the end of the night. And I didn't want you to worry that you smelled like the Swamp, because you don't. You smell yummy, sort of like baby wipes, but in a good way."

I bit my lip and looked down. Stupid-ass cologne.

Ani didn't say anything about my embarrassment. "But then I just realized you don't like mustard on your hot dogs so that probably wasn't very appetizing for you. Sorry." She rooted in her back pocket and pulled out a packet of mints. She unwrapped four of them and popped them into her mouth. She bit down without even sucking on them.

I watched her chew and she offered me the packet. Did this mean she was going to kiss me again? She smiled and unwrapped one of the mints. Her hand shook slightly and I held back a grin. Nervous, like me. She handed me one of the mints. I put it on my tongue.

"Not a biter, huh?" she asked as the mint shrank in my mouth.

"Not with mints," I answered, and then blushed. Tiny beads of sweat formed on my head. Damn bald head showed everything.

She laughed and pulled me up from the table. She linked her fingers behind my neck and drew me toward her. Her tongue slipped into my mouth and she sucked the rest of my mint onto her lips. The bottom dropped out of my stomach. She grinned and started crunching on the mint. I wanted to keep kissing her, but she moved away and I realized we were less than ten feet from a very entertained zoo cashier.

"Let's play a game," she said, directing me toward the large dolphin statue fountain in the center of the zoo. "For every person we see, let's try to figure out where they'll be in ten years."

"Oh-kay."

"Come on. It'll be fun. What about those guys?" she said, and pointed to three guys in baseball caps, big T-shirts, and baggy pants. "Where do you think they'll be in ten years?"

"Prison," I answered.

"What?" She slapped my arm. "What kind of answer is that? Come on, Bumble. Where's your faith in mankind?"

I looked the guys over again. "Well, they could be out on parole by then. They may only be petty criminals."

She opened her mouth but then saw my grin and laughed. Her laughter was more of a guffaw and it wrapped itself around us in a shell of realness. I nearly stumbled.

"What about you? Where are you going to be in ten years?" I asked.

She looked at the cloudy night sky for a second and then shut her eyes, like she was waiting for the answer to rain over her. She took a deep breath and I watched her chest rise. I took a step toward her, but then her eyes popped open and she smiled at me.

"Hopefully not in prison," she said. "I guess . . . I don't really know. I don't need to be famous or anything, but it'd be nice if I could get paid for my art so I don't have to get some crappy job where I'm forced to wear grandma panty hose and answer phones every day. What about you?"

"I don't know. It's hard to think so far ahead. I guess I'll be out of college, but really, I'm not sure what I want to do with my life."

It was a disappointing answer, but Ani didn't seem to mind. She nodded and rubbed the top of my head like it was a Magic 8 Ball, taking all the seriousness out of our conversation. I ducked out of her reach and she jumped on me from behind, tackling me onto a patch of grass and dragging her tongue up the back of my head. I flipped her and straddled her hips.

Her teeth bit her bottom lip and she gave me an evil grin.

"This is a bit of a compromising position, Ben. I think you better hop up before you embarrass yourself and pop wood in front of half the zoo," she said, and bucked her hips.

I leaped to my feet and she followed, grabbing my hand again. Being with Ani was like being smacked upside the head. There wasn't anything she wouldn't say. It was like hanging out in the locker room with a bunch of guys, only she was wrapped up in a package of gorgeous.

We played the "Where Will They Be in Ten Years" game for a little bit longer, but when I kept answering "prison" to all the people she pointed out, she got frustrated and quit. I didn't want to ruin her fun, but really, these people were hanging at the zoo on a Saturday night; if that didn't point to a future with the Department of Corrections, I didn't know what did.

Since she ate most of our dinner, she bought me a lemon ice. She took small bites from me as we walked. Her tongue darted out of her mouth, and I distracted myself by reciting names of Olympic swimmers in my head so I didn't have to tie a coat around my waist to get to the exit. Who knew sharing a tiny wooden spoon could be so frickin' sexy? She talked me into taking a Motor Safari train ride and nestled beneath my arm as we listened to the corny guided tour of the zoo. I closed my eyes and wished the night would never end.

5

"I'm going swimming at the lake," I told my brother when I found him in his room early the next morning. "Do you wanna come?"

He looked up from his clarinet. "Is anyone else going?"

"No. I'm training." The lake was hard to swim; perfect for intense workouts. The current could be fierce and even after a full summer, the temperature bit into me like an icy dagger. But nothing helped clear my head more.

He leaned over and placed his clarinet carefully in its case, then set the case on the only empty shelf in his otherwise mess of a room. Michael wasn't an intentional slob; he just didn't care enough about neatness to pay attention. "Can I pick the music for the ride there?"

I released a breath. "Okay. But nothing that's gonna make

me fall asleep. I'm working on about four hours here, shrimp."

He grinned. "Yeah. I heard you come in. After curfew. I wanted to talk to you, but I was too tired. Did Dad say anything?"

"Not really. He smelled my breath and told me to go to bed."

The zoo closed at nine, but Ani wanted me to drive her to the city to see some band. After ninety minutes of aimlessly searching for an all-ages club that Ani couldn't remember the name or address of, we ended up parked in an alley, making out. My lips still buzzed from the taste of her. And I had no idea how she was going to explain the stubble burn on her cheeks to her mom.

"Guess you had fun, then?" Michael said.

I ruffled his hair and grabbed him in a headlock. "Guess so."

My body tensed up the minute I entered the water, and I had to take a bunch of short breaths to acclimate to the cold. Michael sat on the cement drop-off playing his handheld game and ignoring the people on the beach fifty feet away. After my body got used to the water, I dove under and held my breath as long as I could.

When I emerged, I saw Michael had put his game to the side. Relief flashed across his face. He waved and went back to playing. My arms pulled me into an easy freestyle stroke. Two minutes later, I started to really pump. In the water, thoughts passed over me in a way that made me feel invincible. Like everything I worried about was stupid and would work itself out if I just let go.

Thirty minutes into my swim, my pace was steady, but I could tell from my breathing that I was moving faster than usual. Arms reaching, legs kicking, every pull became a rhythm in my head. *Ani. Ani. Ani.*

"Dude, seriously, if you make me drink again, I'm gonna hurl," Kevin slurred from across the crappy green card table in his basement. The paneled walls around us were covered with the faded posters of hip-hop stars Kevin had hung when we were in fifth grade. He must have put "Eminem radio" into his playlist because every white-guy rapper I could think of was shuffling through the speakers in the background.

"You were the one who wanted to play Asshole. If you can't take the heat, don't suggest the game," I said, and gave Ani a grin. Her face flushed and my stomach flipped. It'd been two weeks since the night at the zoo. Two weeks of holding her hand in the hall and making out in my Jeep and texting late at night.

I'd had a bit of a high at the beginning with Morgan, but with Ani, it was so much more. I'd only ever seen Morgan at parties or when other people were around. She'd liked us to be out together, but I guess I wasn't interesting enough for her on my own. With Ani, I sort of hated when other people were around because they interfered with our vibe together, interrupted time for me to learn everything about her.

Friday at lunch, Kevin called me pathetic and demanded I pull out my man card and drink with him or he'd cut me off as a friend. He wouldn't. We'd known each other for too long and Kevin respected breasts enough not to interfere with a guy's opportunity to spend time with them. So I compromised and brought Ani with me.

"I only suggested the game because the guy who told me about it made it seem fun. I thought we'd all take turns and it'd be an excellent drinking game. But, dude, I keep being the asshole, which means I've been drinking more and longer than any of you chumps." Kevin let out a huge burp.

Ani shook her head and smirked at Kevin. "You're fine. You obviously are sober enough to complain. I think it's time for another Social."

"Argh," Kevin mumbled, putting his beer to his lips. "And that's another thing, how come we're having so many Socials? Let me win already so I can be president."

"No, that's cheating." I tried not to laugh. Kevin was never going to be president. As the asshole, he couldn't stop drinking during the Social until the rest of us stopped. I noticed Ani had pretended to drink a lot during the night, but she was barely swallowing anything. Poor Kevin.

"I said Social." Ani banged her hand against the table and we all raised our cans and toasted. I looked at Ani's friend Kate. Her dark hair was superstraight in the weird way girls make it look like it was ironed. She sipped her drink and scrunched her face. Her skin was starting to look a bit pasty. I hoped it was just the bad fluorescent lighting.

My eyes rested on Ani. She wasn't totally wasted, but definitely had a strong buzz going on. I pointed to Kate's pale face and Ani sprang from her chair, knocking it over and laughing.

"I think we should be heading home," she said.

Crap. I hadn't meant for her to leave. I'd thought maybe she could help Kate go lie down somewhere.

"You just got here. We still have at least five beers left," I protested like some bumbling idiot who'd never had girls over before.

Why'd she want to take off? It was fun playing drinking games in Kevin's basement, and I'd originally hoped Kevin and Kate might get along so Ani and I could have some time by ourselves.

Too bad Kate took one look at Kevin when he opened the door with a huge flapping wave of his arms and mumbled, "Oh, great, the psycho with the pliers."

The guy would never be able to shake that story.

Kevin had gotten drunk on grape juice and Everclear one night our sophomore year and decided to remove his own braces with his dad's pliers. I thought it was frickin' hilarious seeing him walk around with a bunch of wires coming out of his mouth, but the sober people at the party were disgusted, especially when he accidentally pulled out one of his teeth along with the brace.

Apparently Kevin's reputation still preceded him, and Kate had slid her chair close to Ani's when we all sat down to play. It didn't look like I'd even get to second base with how much the girls were laughing and snorting when they stood up to leave.

"We got here like four hours ago," Ani said when she was composed enough to answer me. "And you'll see me tomorrow at the swim meet."

I grinned. I'd never had a girlfriend go to one of my meets before. It wasn't even a real meet. It was an intersquad preseason competition. Still, I'd been pretty nervous asking Ani, but she'd agreed without bitching or holding it over me. I loved that about her.

"Aw, you're going to his swim meet?" Kate said. "That's so cute. Are you going to hold up a sign that says 'Number One Beez Fan'?"

"No," Ani said through another bout of snorting laughter. "I was thinking something more like 'Hold On to Your Honey, Here Comes Beez.'"

Kevin started to laugh. "No. Wait. How about 'Mind Your Own Beezness'?" He doubled over in hysterics.

Kate, Ani, and I exchanged looks. Kevin laughed for thirty

more seconds while we stared at him. Finally his chuckles died down.

"That's not even funny," Kate deadpanned. "That might be the worst pun ever." She turned to me. "We need to go. Ani told her mom we'd be home by midnight." She shifted her focus to Kevin. "Unless you're thinking of waxing your chest hair or something. Because I'd break curfew for that."

I bit the inside of my cheek to keep from laughing. Obviously Kate wasn't that wasted if she could still bust Kevin's balls. Ani snorted again. Kevin opened and closed his mouth three times, but Kate held up her hand.

"Don't even try. You're way too drunk to pull off a good comeback."

Kevin looked at me and I shook my head. He loved a challenge, but I didn't think his alcohol-induced charm would work on Kate.

"Why don't I help you get your coats?" I asked. I stood up on wobbly legs and placed my hand against the wall to steady myself.

"You're such a charmer, Beez," Kevin said, and faced the girls. "That's from his dad's side." He burped to emphasize his point. Classy. "Don't let him fool you. He acts sort of white, but he's a total Haitian gentleman about shit like holding doors and getting coats."

"Don't be a douche," I said, shoving Kevin.

Ani put her hands on her hips and looked me up and down. "Is this offer to help because you're thinking you might get some?"

Kevin choked on a sip of beer. I looked at my feet before anyone could see me blush. I liked Ani's directness, but sometimes she went overboard.

"Beezus," she said, and I met her eyes. "I'm kinda tipsy and I bet you taste like the bottom of a garbage can. If you want to feel me up, okay, but you'll probably mess it up with your drunken gropes, and I wouldn't say that's exactly good times, you follow?"

"I'm not drunk," I said. Why was I defending myself in front of Kevin and Kate? I looked like a novice who'd never touched a boob before.

Ani laughed but then took my hand. "Okay, okay, come on."

Kevin stood up, teetering like he wasn't going to be able to take three steps without passing out. I originally thought it was funny we all kept pretending to drink so he'd lose and be the asshole in the game, but I hoped it didn't mean I was going to be cleaning up his puke and putting him to bed later.

"Don't worry. I'll entertain Kate," he said.

She snorted. "How? Is there a set of pliers down here?"

Ani and I both chuckled. We moved to the bottom of the stairs and Ani did a weird girl signal to Kate that I gathered meant "give us a few minutes."

She walked upstairs with me on her heels. I'd never been so into a girl. I reached out to put my hands on her waist but she wiggled away from me.

"No offense, Romeo, but I don't want you pulling me down the stairs if you stumble, and I sure as hell don't feel solid enough on my feet to help keep you steady."

My hands dropped. Ani looked back at me and gave me a half smile. My heart squeezed. I was in deep.

Kevin's parents had gone away for the weekend and had left him with his older brother, Matt, who'd basically told him he didn't give a shit what Kevin did, but he better not ruin the house because he was on his own to fix anything he broke. Then Matt headed out the door and Kevin busted into his dad's beer stash and invited us over.

Ani led me to the bathroom and rifled through the drawers and cabinets. She finally found a tube of toothpaste and swiped some on her finger, using it to scrub her teeth. She handed the toothpaste to me without a word. I mirrored her movements. Ani's tongue licked its way across her teeth and I stifled a groan and focused on finger brushing. We both rinsed our mouths with water. She hopped onto the counter and pulled me in between her legs.

"Okay, that's better. You can kiss me now."

I moved toward her and bumped into her nose because we both tilted in the same direction. Very smooth. She put her hands on my cheeks and tilted me the other way. She tasted like new toothpaste and old beer and I shifted closer to her, my hands fumbling up her sides.

Ani giggled. "That tickles and I thought I covered how you should wait to touch my boobs until we're more sober."

Ani seemed perfectly sober to me, and even the buzz in my head had pretty much cleared up once I'd kissed her. But there was no sense arguing once she made up her mind. My hands dropped to her waist and she licked my bottom lip. I nipped at her and when she opened her mouth, I stuck my tongue in deep. Her legs linked behind me and I got instantly hard.

My hands curled into her hips and I kept telling myself not to move them. Ani shifted against me and must have felt me pressed against her thigh because she sort of laugh-snorted. I pulled away and looked down.

"Sorry, Bumble. I don't mean to laugh. It's flattering, really."

I was such an ass. I couldn't even control myself. I might have given up on the whole thing, but I had the liquid confidence of four beers rushing through me, and I wasn't going to let embarrassment keep me from kissing Ani.

"I have . . . I'm just . . . I really like you," I said finally. Sheesh. Frickin' novice. I scrubbed my hand over my face.

She ran her hands over my back and pulled me closer into her.

"You're shaking," she whispered, and I looked down at

51

my hands, which were trembling a bit. Probably because they were losing circulation gripping her jeans to keep them from roaming anywhere else.

"I don't want to stop," I said. Kate and Kevin waited for us, probably having an awkward conversation and staring at the basement door, but I didn't really care. I wanted to inhale Ani. The starkness of the truth sat between us and I wondered if Ani understood all that it meant.

"Just one more minute," she answered, and tugged me back into her. The stones from the pendant on her necklace pressed into my chest as she pulled me tighter.

After too short a time, she stopped me with a little shove to my chest. Her eyes were sort of glassy and she breathed heavily. I hoped it was from the kisses and not the beer.

She looked me over carefully. "That was sexy. I probably should have let you touch my boobs. Oh well, next time." She pushed me farther back and hopped off the counter. "I've got to go rescue Kate. She'll never let me hear the end of it in school on Monday if I don't. I'll see you tomorrow."

6

My eyes scanned the crowd of parents and students for the seventh time in five minutes. Ani wasn't there yet. Hell. I hoped she wasn't bailing. I didn't want to be mad at her. Even if she had a good reason to miss my meet, I'd hold a grudge. I knew myself enough to know that a no-show would bug the crap out of me.

The speaker buzzed to life behind me and called for my event. I grabbed my goggles and headed toward the edge of the pool. One last look into the stands. Someone was pushing through the last row. Ani. Face flushed, hair falling out of the ponytail she wore. She stood on the top bleacher and lifted a pink neon poster board painted with a giant bumblebee in a swim cap. My face split in half. I waved to her and she dropped the poster and blew me a kiss.

I almost pretended to grab it out of the air, but I stopped myself. Yes. I was that close to having my man card revoked. I waved again and adjusted the goggles onto my eyes. My heart was pumping harder than it had at last year's regionals.

The starter buzzed and I dove into the pool like I was flying. My arms and legs moved in sync with the drumming of my chest and before I could even think about the swimmers in the other lanes, I was being pulled from the water and slapped on the back. Cheers from the crowd roared in my ears.

The coach's enthusiastic shouts passed through me. My gaze moved to Ani, dancing on the bleacher, clapping and smiling at me. She did a mock salute and winked at me. Coach continued his cheerful monologue. I looked at the scoreboard on the wall and blinked, rubbed my eyes, looked again. I'd just beat the school record for the fifty-meter freestyle.

Gazing back at Ani, I held a finger up and mouthed the words "Wait for me."

She nodded and mouthed back, "Always."

"Guess who?" I said, sneaking up behind Ani in the art room after swim practice a week later.

"Um, let me think . . . is it the dork I'm dating, who thinks Guess Who games are still cute?"

I dropped my hands and stepped away from her. She was right. What the hell was going on with me?

"Aw, Bumble, your feelings are hurt," she said, taking my hand. "I didn't mean to call you a dork. Lots of people still play Guess Who. I totally saw someone doing it last week at the library during Toddler Story Time." She giggled and snaked her arms around my neck.

I shook her off and took a step back. I tried to keep my face stony, but Ani pouted and tugged on my ears so I gave up and laughed at myself.

"What are you working on?" I asked, pointing to the painting behind her.

"Do you like it?" she said, and beamed at me. She was like a proud little girl showing off her new purple Rollerblades. Frickin' adorable.

I studied the painting, tilting my head to both sides. "It's not bad, but I think your mom is a bit meatier than that."

Her painting was of a skeletal woman with crazy curly hair and dark, deep-set eyes. A large necklace of handcuffs circled her throat and a cigarette was dangling from her mouth, the smoke pouring through her ears and nose.

"Very funny," she said, and shifted the painting to the corner before covering it carefully with a cloth.

"The handcuff necklace is kind of interesting. Maybe you could start making those instead of the trees?"

She fingered the pendant on her neck. Green today. "Might be kind of bulky. And doesn't exactly send the same message."

"Seriously," I said, grabbing her backpack and throwing it over my shoulder, "the painting's amazing. But I'm kinda simple about this stuff. What's it supposed to mean?"

She wiped her hands on her jeans and pulled her backpack from my shoulder, slinging it over her arm.

"Well, you were actually sort of right. It *is* my mom, chained down by a world in which single moms barely make ends meet while deadbeat dads can go off on their merry way and ignore any responsibility."

"Umm . . ."

Ani crossed her arms and tilted her head. Damn girl tests.

"Men suck," I said with an even voice. How else was I supposed to answer? Ani almost never talked about her dad and I didn't want to push her about it. I figured she talked to Kate since it was more girl stuff anyways.

She gave me a huge grin. "Yes, they definitely suck. Now, why don't you buy me a Slurpee and I'll read to you from Inga Muscio's *Cunt*?"

"What?"

She chuckled. "*Cunt*. You'll love it."

"If I have to listen to that, you better be the one buying Slurpees today."

"Deal."

. . .

"Where to?" Ani asked as she slipped into my Jeep three days later.

I shifted my eyes to the side and glanced at her bare legs. Even after almost a month, I couldn't stop staring at them. My heart thunked in my chest and my palms felt like an overly enthusiastic poodle had licked them.

"Beez." Ani snapped her fingers. "I'm up here."

I grinned. "Sorry. Nice legs."

"Are you going to sit here all night admiring them or are we actually getting food?" Ani crossed one smooth, tan thigh over the other. I raised an eyebrow.

"You're teasing me?"

She smiled and I lost my breath. Three and a half weeks and my lungs still didn't work right around her.

"Dinner, Beez. I'm starving. Where are you taking me?"

I gripped the steering wheel with my slick palms and forced myself to move. "Zoo."

She laughed. "Again? You're taking me to dinner at the zoo again? If I didn't know any better, I'd think it was becoming our place."

"I like your mustardy kisses," I said.

She belly laughed and it circled around me, through me, and made me want to pull the Jeep over again so I could make out with her. She leaned in and squeezed my shoulder. "You're a surprisingly good boyfriend. I wouldn't have guessed it when we first met."

"Um, thanks?"

She sat back into the crappy vinyl of my bucket seats and sighed in the way girls do when they're thinking about serious stuff. "Not everyone likes mustard," she said as she looked out the window. She turned back to me. "I'm glad you do."

"Is this your Ani way of telling me you really like me?" *Please say yes.* Christ, don't let me be the moron who's fallen too hard, too fast for a girl who only half likes me.

She shook her head. "Of course it isn't. I think you've known me long enough to know I'm not that subtle."

I snorted and coughed.

She swatted me. "Shut up. You think my honesty's adorable." Adorable and amazing and like no girl I'd ever met.

"So?" I asked her, and hated that my voice sounded needy. Idiot move, but there was no turning back now. I pulled the Jeep to the side of the road and stared at her.

She licked her lips and blinked. Why do girls do this? Always with the lip licking. Surely this was some ploy they learned in the girls' locker room to turn us inside out.

"I like you," she said, and didn't break eye contact with me. "Just as much as you like me. Maybe more." She grinned and the breath locked in my throat again. "Now can we get a move on here? I'm starving, and sitting on the side of the road is not getting you any closer to mustardy kisses."

Ani hated going to movies. She shot me down every time I even suggested it.

"I don't get to tease you or make fun of your little quirks when we're in a movie theater," she whined. We were in my Jeep heading to the cemetery on a Sunday afternoon so I could teach her how to drive stick shift.

"And that would be the whole point. You owe me a make-out session in the movie theater. I've had to put up with weeks of your teasing. Plus, I'm teaching you stick—that at least earns me some chest action." I paused for a second, but her smile didn't break. I was still surprised at how much I could say to Ani. I didn't have to second-guess myself or worry I'd put my foot in my mouth.

"Nice try. You *offered* to help. And you might as well admit you love my awesome monologues on our dates. You'd be lost without them. I've seen you with those guys after swim practice. All you do is grunt at each other."

"Really?" I asked, turning into the cemetery entrance.

"Yes, it's like this secret language of boys made up of grunting, hooting, and shoving. Maybe you could give me some sort of decoder so I could figure out what it all means."

I parked the car and turned to her. "I'm not sure I know you well enough to let you in on our secrets yet. You've only been to one swim meet after all. And it wasn't even an official competition."

She leaned toward me. "I might be able to make it worth your while," she said, and rubbed the top of my head. I'd gotten used to her petting. In this twisted way, I sort of craved it.

"Really?" I asked, my throat going a bit dry.

"I've been known to be very persuasive."

She was kidding, but I swallowed hard anyway. I'd been thinking of having sex with Ani since the first day at her house. Sort of pathetic. Really pathetic, actually. My parents would kill me, or at the very least give me an endless lecture about "personal responsibility." But with Ani's legs and how she talked and the way she made me feel, my brain kept latching onto the idea of the two of us together.

I cleared my throat. "I can't just give this information out to anyone. You'd have to prove yourself worthy. I mean, there was a reason they separated the boys and girls in health class in fifth grade."

Ani cracked an even bigger smile. "Is that when you guys learned how to grunt? Well, shit. All we learned about were periods and how to put in tampons the right way."

I held my hands up. "Gross. Too much information."

Ani shifted closer to me. She batted her eyelashes and turned on what she called her vixen charm. "So how do I prove myself worthy?"

I looked her up and down. Should I say it? It'd be too soon, but everything was so comfortable with Ani. Blunt and direct. "You could, uh, sleep with me."

Ani pulled back. Her face closed up. Damn. I knew it was too soon. God, I was such an ass.

"Forget it. I didn't mean that. I . . . uh . . . You don't have to prove anything with me. To me. Whatever." Aw, crap. I was babbling like a girl.

Ani crossed her arms and I tried hard not to look at her cleavage. Stupid girl shirts with their low-cut necks. Her necklace hung just above her boobs so I focused there. Blue stones woven together with wire.

"You want to have sex with me?"

I scratched the back of my neck and looked at her face. Not mad, more curious. "Well, yeah. I mean, not if you're not ready. But I think things are going pretty good between us, so I thought maybe . . ."

"It's pretty early, Bumble. I'm not really a jump-in-the-sack-after-the-first-month kind of girl."

"I didn't think you were," I said. I was glad she wasn't. It sucks for guys to think about their girlfriends being with other guys.

She tapped her finger on her chin. I shifted in my seat and played with the keys. I looked at an old Slurpee cup forgotten in the cup holder. There were fast food wrappers on the floor at Ani's feet. My car was an embarrassing vortex of crap. I was a dirtbag. What girl could think about sex sitting in my disgusting car?

"Let me get back to you on that one," she said finally.

I let out a breath. What the hell was I thinking bringing this up now?

"I'll still teach you to drive, though."

She laughed. "God, I hope so. I'd feel terrible if you had to drive the entire time on our road trip next summer."

"We're going on a road trip?" And she was talking about us next summer? Sweet.

"Of course. After graduation. After you get your swim scholarship. We're going camping across the Midwest. And then we're going to visit the house where they filmed *A Christmas Story*," she said. Her energy was like a hot shower after running a marathon in an ice storm.

"*A Christmas Story*? That Ralphie movie?"

"Yes. The house is in Ohio. It's right by the world's biggest candy store. It'll be great. We can bring your brother if you want." I loved Michael, but there was no way in hell I was taking him camping with me and Ani.

"I think Michael'll be busy with other things."

Ani grinned at me. "Uh-huh. Well, road trip with just us, then."

"Yep. Just us."

I pulled the keys out of the ignition and handed them to her. She hopped out of the car and was at my door before I could even get out. She leaned in and kissed me. My sappy heart thundered in my chest, and even though it was barely fall, I wished next summer would come soon.

7

"Are you sure your mom's not going to be back until late?" I asked for the forty-seventh time while Ani straddled my lap in her jeans and bra. The window in her room was open, and I was sitting on the edge of her unmade bed. I'd come over to help her hang one of her paintings in her room. It was late October and I loved the way her skin got goose bumps from the cool fall air.

"Ben," she said, nibbling tiny kisses along my jaw, "I'm pretty sure she knows we're sleeping together. She's probably known since the first time."

I pulled her away from me and looked into her big eyes. "Really? But why would she know anything? We've always been at my house when my parents were gone or in my Jeep." After I'd cleaned it out, Ani didn't mind having sex in the Jeep. Which was good because our space options were pretty limited.

"Oh my God, you're such a girl. Why do you think? 'Cause I told her, of course," Ani said, and started back with her maddening kisses down my neck.

"You told her?" I pushed her back slightly and set her onto her lumpy green comforter beside me. "Ani, what the hell? When did you tell her?"

"After the cemetery. When you first asked me and I told you I had to think about it."

"That was more than two weeks ago. How come you didn't tell me anything about it before now?"

Ani took a deep breath and pulled her shirt back on. I almost reached out to stop her, but it wouldn't have made any difference. I'd killed the mood of our hookup with my worrying. I fisted my hand in frustration.

"Ben, my mom's not like your parents. She's a single mom who teaches art. When you asked me to have sex with you, I thought I should get her opinion on the whole thing. I knew I wanted to, but we'd only been going out for, like, a month and sometimes my judgment gets a little skewed by your sexy baldness." Ani ran her hand over my scalp and tingles crept down my spine.

"So you just put it out there?" I asked, hooking my finger into her belt loop and pulling her back onto my lap.

"I figured my mom might help me see through all the hormone drama so I could look at things rationally."

"And what'd she say?" I slipped my hands beneath the edge of her T-shirt and traced my fingers over her hip bones. I had a hard time keeping my hands off her when we were together. We hadn't even had sex that many times, but it didn't matter. I couldn't stop touching her wherever we were. Her body rocked.

"She told me she thought it was too soon. She said she liked you, but she didn't think dating you for a month was a long enough time to figure out if I wanted to give you that part of me."

"Well, then, how come you slept with me?"

Ani tugged on my ears and pulled my face up to meet her gaze. "'Cause of your sexy baldness. I couldn't help myself. I told my mom afterward and she said she was disappointed, but she's a mom, that's what she's supposed to say. The day after, she put a box of condoms on my bed."

"Annika, you're gonna be the death of me," I said as I slid my hands underneath her shirt to unhook her bra.

"No, I won't. I'm the girl of your dreams," she said, and licked the ticklish spot beneath my ear.

I pulled away from her long enough to remove both our shirts and flipped her beneath me. "Yes. Yes, you are."

I switched off the knobs of the icy shower in the locker room and snagged the towel from the bench next to me. Most of the other swimmers had already taken off, but Kevin and I had stayed longer to practice our transitions during the relay. Official swim team would be starting soon and my times were the best they'd ever been.

"So Morgan totally accosted me in the hall the other day," Kevin said as I opened my locker and dug around for my clothes.

"Yeah?"

"Yeah, she was all, 'How are things with Beez and Ani? Is he still into her?' Blah. Blah. Blah. Blah. Bitch and moan."

I grabbed my T-shirt and pulled it over my head. "Why? She doesn't think she still has a chance with me, does she?" Christ, how many times did Morgan need to be hit over the head?

"Well, she doesn't anymore. I told her you two were going at it like rabbits and that pretty much shut her up."

"Douche bag." I threw my wet towel at Kevin's head. "You can't get involved in girls' catty games. And don't ever tell Morgan about what I'm doing with Ani."

"Whatever. Ani would eat Morgan alive."

I smiled. She totally would. Morgan wouldn't know what the hell to do with the Ani package.

"Still. It's not Morgan's business and you shouldn't be saying shit about me and Ani."

"But you are tapping that, right?"

I shook my head at Kevin. "Tapping that? Seriously, dude,

you have to stop watching so much MTV. You're white, get over yourself."

Kevin laughed. He didn't care. We'd had the "you're a hip-hop poseur" conversation at least fifteen times before. Still didn't stop him from peppering his conversation with references to "the hood" and "my niggas."

"We should all go skiing over winter break," Kevin said.

"I don't know about that." I didn't want to tell him my plans for winter break included spending as much time as I could with Ani.

"Come on. Ani can bring Kate. I'm trying to be flexible here. I haven't once given you a hard time about you breaking our 'bros before hos' motto."

"You mean *your* 'bros before hos' motto?" I asked with a grin.

"Dude. That's a universal guy motto. And I haven't said anything about how I barely see you anymore."

I hit him on the back of the head. "That's because it'd be a lie. You see me all the time. Ani would never ask me to choose her over you. And she'd never throw over Kate for me. She's the queen of 'sisters before misters.'"

Kevin laughed. "She might be, but you totally aren't. And listen, dude, I don't care. She's hot and you're into her. But still, it wouldn't kill you to invite me to hang with you over winter break."

"'Kay. Message received. You can hang with us."

I slid on my pants and shoved my feet into my sneakers. Kevin bounced on his feet next to me.

"I can drive home, if you want," he offered. I hated to tell him no when he got so excited, but the guy was about the worst driver ever. I'd partnered with him in driver's ed and learned to expect a near accident every time it was his turn behind the wheel.

"No one touches my baby but me," I said, feeling slightly guilty about how much time Ani had spent practicing stick in the past two weeks.

"So protective of all your girls," Kevin said, and snorted.

I pulled out my keys and gestured to the locker room door. "Shut up. Let's go."

"What's that?" Kevin pointed to the triangular stone attached to my keys.

Heat swept up my neck to my ears. "Nothing. It's just something Ani made for me. A key ring."

Kevin howled. "Did she give it to you right after you gave her your class ring? Jesus, dude, this is worse than I thought."

"What? It's cool. Look, it has this tree in it. Ani wears them all the time. They sort of have this special meaning for her."

Kevin slapped me on the back. "Bro, this is seriously the most pathetic I've ever seen you. Even at the beginning with Morgan, you weren't this whipped. I mean, really? A key ring with a tree in it?"

"Shut the hell up. You're just jealous because you don't have anyone to spend time with but your hand."

Kevin grabbed his bag. "Dude, I'd never be jealous of a key ring with a tree in it."

I shrugged. "Unless it came attached to a girl with nice legs and a great smile who showed up to your meets with a pink sign."

He held the locker room door open for me. "The legs I'd take, but all the rest of it, pass. I'm not cut out for girlfriend drama. That's all you."

I clenched the key ring in my hand and thought of Ani's excited face when she gave it to me. How she'd held my hand for too long before pressing the stone into my palm. How she'd babbled about connection and the universe bringing us together at the right time. How she kissed me afterward like she wanted to kiss me for the rest of my life. Yeah, she was worth every bit of shit Kevin gave me.

"So girls' weekend?" I said to Ani over the phone later that night. I was lying on my bed, trying to gather the energy to get some homework done.

"Yes. Tomorrow night, movie with Mom. Saturday with Kate."

"How come you'll see a movie with your mom but not me?"

Michael's clarinet warm-up seeped through the wall between our rooms. I shifted my position on the pillow and stretched my legs over the edge of the bed to swing myself up.

"Mom's already heard all my stories. I don't have that much to say to her. Especially since you got all prickly about me telling her about you."

I laughed. "Well, Ani, there is a limit."

"So you say. Anyway, Mom knows everything about me. But I still have lots of things to say to you."

"Yeah. Like what?"

She laughed a little. "I don't know. Don't put me on the spot like that. I'll probably think of something as soon as we hang up."

"Okay. I gotta do some homework anyway. But call me this weekend."

"Of course, Bumble. You know you *are* invited to the party on Saturday."

Raver party? Pass. "Yeah, I don't think so. You all can go ahead and have your girl time."

"Ha. We will."

"But if it sucks, you can call me. Or you know . . ."

"Aww, you're gonna miss me, baby? Don't worry, I'll call. Actually, I'll do even better. I'll plan something for the two of us on Sunday."

Family commitment. Mom's voice bled into my brain, but it was overshadowed by the promise of a full Ani day.

"It'll be fun. And different," Ani teased.

"Yeah," I said. "I'll have to juggle some things, but I can

probably swing that. You better make it worth my while, though. I'm talking a real plan. That involves food and doesn't involve me handing over the keys to my Jeep so you can practice driving."

"A real plan. I'm on it. I'll let you know details when I have them ironed out. Now hang up."

I barked out a laugh. "What if I don't want to?"

"Michael's playing. Go listen to him. I'll talk to you tomorrow."

"Good night."

"Good night, Bumble, I love you."

Before I could say anything, she clicked off. *I love you.* Of course she'd say it on the phone like it was no big deal. And of course she wouldn't ask for it back. That was how Ani rolled. But my stomach flipped over and I felt like I had to pee in the good way that happens when something incredible has occurred. *I love you.* She'd said it first. I flipped open my phone and quickly texted her.

I love you too.

I stared at my phone and less than a minute later her response pinged.

I know.

8

I'd checked my phone at least three dozen times before finally seeing Ani's number pop up.

"What the fuck? Where have you been? Why didn't you text me when you got to Kate's last night?"

I didn't want to sound like an asshole, but she was three hours late for lunch and I was starting to feel like a chump sitting around waiting for my girlfriend. I'd blown my family off and was missing extra time in the pool because Ani wanted to have a picnic. Her big plan. Plus, her mom had called and asked where she was, and I had to lie and say I was on my way to pick her up at Kate's house.

"It's not Ani."

"Kate?"

"Yeah, look, you've got to come to county hospital."

"What? What's happened? Where's Ani?"

"She's here. But listen, she didn't want me to call you. Or her mom. And they said they couldn't contact anyone without her permission. But you need to come."

I scrambled around my room, searching for my keys. "I'm on my way. What the hell happened?" I couldn't swallow. My mouth had gone completely dry.

"I'm not really sure. I mean, I was at that party with her last night. There were lots of guys there. I didn't think she was drinking that much, but then she started acting sort of crazy. Her words were a little slurred and she kept leaning on people. Mostly the guys. She sounded like she was really drunk, but I swear, I was pretty sober and she didn't seem like she had more than two or three drinks."

I closed my eyes and shook my head. Ani was at the hospital? This wasn't happening. My hands were shaking so badly I could barely get the key in the ignition of my Jeep.

"Does she have alcohol poisoning or something?" I asked, but my voice sounded like it came from someone else.

"No. It's not like that. Just come, Ben. She needs you even if she isn't saying it."

I drove so recklessly on the way there, I knew I was going to get at least two of those red-light photo-enforcement tickets. Everything seemed loud and bright as I slammed my way into the ER, where Kate sat wringing her hands around a bottle of water. County. The hospital of crappy service, long wait times, and the incessant smell of sickness. Why had Ani gone there?

"Start at the beginning," I said as calmly as I could. "Where's Ani now?"

"They're prepping her for a surgical procedure."

"What?" I shouted, and the nurse from the triage desk glared at me.

"Okay, just sit down and listen," Kate said, tugging me into the pea-green plastic chair next to her. "You knew I went with Ani to that party, right?"

I nodded. The party Ani invited me to, but I passed on. It was at some random house west of the city with a bunch of those raver freaks, and I hated house music.

"Well, like I said, I thought she only had maybe two drinks, but then she started acting all nuts, like table dancing in the kitchen and being superclingy to everyone."

"Table dancing? What? She was table dancing?"

"Shh . . . just listen. I'm not going to be able to do this if you interrupt."

I swallowed past the lump in my throat and nodded.

"Anyways, I asked if she was okay, and she pointed to this group of guys and told me she was going to get with them. I told her we should call you, but then this guy sort of pushed me away and then she was kissing him."

"What? She was table dancing *and* kissing another guy?

75

Why *didn't* you call me?" My head was spinning. Too much. Too fast. I couldn't digest everything Kate was saying.

Kate looked at her hands clutched tightly around the water bottle. An ambulance sounded in the distance. "I thought maybe you two had a fight and Ani was rebounding. That she just didn't want to talk to me about it. Like she was letting off steam or something."

"She said girls' night," I choked out.

"Yeah. She was staying over at my house, but it was a party. And you *were* invited. Why didn't you come?"

I shook my head but couldn't speak. Kate's words ripped through me like a machete. My eyes focused on a thin old woman across the room, her yellow skin shaking as she hacked into a handkerchief.

"I kept telling her I'd take her home, but she said she was fine," Kate continued. "That she knew what she was doing. I didn't really know what to do, but she told me to back the hell out of her life."

"Did you know the guy? The one she was kissing?" I asked.

"No, he was with a big group, and they were at the party before we even got there. I didn't recognize any of them, but there were a lot of people we didn't know."

"Did she leave with that guy?" I asked weakly. I was tripped up on the idea of Ani kissing someone else. There was more to all this, but I couldn't work through what Kate was describing. It wasn't my Ani.

"No, she went upstairs. But with a bunch of them, you know?" Kate's voice shook. "Some girls went with them too. I thought maybe they were going to play spin the bottle or something. I didn't notice, but I guess some of them came back down later."

I shut my eyes. *Please, God, don't let this be real. Don't let this be what it seems.* Something inside me snapped and I turned on Kate. Venom ran through me.

"Why didn't you go with her upstairs? Don't you girls have some sort of buddy system at parties? What kind of shitty friend lets a drunk girl disappear with a bunch of guys?"

"Fuck you. She told me to stay out of her business and she wasn't drinking that much. How was I supposed to know? She was with a *bunch* of guys. I didn't know what was going to happen."

"What did happen, Kate? Why's she going into surgery?"

Kate's fingers started to peel off the wrapper of the water bottle. Her nails scraped at the glue. I put my hand over hers. She looked up at me through tears. She tried to take a deep breath but choked. She wiped her face and shifted closer to me.

"I found her about an hour and a half later. She was passed out. I tried to wake her up, but she was really out of it and said she didn't feel good. I got someone to help me carry her to the car. I took her home and put her to bed. When she woke up this morning, she told me she thought she'd been raped."

Everything froze. No sound. No smell. No feeling in my body. Just a moment of blackness before a shattering crack, and my world reconfiguring itself.

"Jesus, where the hell were you when that was happening?" I screamed, and jumped up. I thought I might be sick.

"Where the hell were *you*?" she screamed back at me, and her eyes flooded with more tears.

The short, overweight triage nurse came over to us and told us to lower our voices or take our conversation outside. I sat back down next to Kate and put my head in my hands.

I was shaking so badly the chair squeaked. "Why's she going into surgery?" It hurt my stomach to ask.

"Well, it's not exactly surgery. They're not in an operating room or anything. They called it a procedure. They're just giving her a local anesthetic to numb her."

"Why, Kate?" What the hell else was she afraid to tell me?

Her hands twisted again on the bottle. "Earlier, the doctor was doing this rape kit. They have to do it to collect evidence. Ani wanted me to stay in the room with her. There was a rape counselor in there too. But when they tried to take samples or whatever, Ani started screaming so loud. Like some kind of wounded animal. She kept yelling that it hurt, it hurt. I thought at first it was because she had this little tear on the outside they needed to stitch up. But then the doctor said he felt something inside of her. He couldn't get it out. So they did an ultrasound to see what it was."

I couldn't breathe. Each new word Kate spoke was like a fist to my gut, hammering into me again and again. I looked at her, afraid to ask.

"It was a lighter, Ben. Whoever did it left a lighter inside of her."

I shook my head too long and the room got blurry. *Lighter. Lighter Lighter.* The word skipped through my mind. I covered my ears and willed myself to move. I slammed out the door and buckled to the ground. My fingers scraped the sidewalk. I buried my head in my knees and tears dampened my jeans. My insides cracked and I curled into a ball to hold myself together. Seconds passed, then minutes. Finally I looked at the cold, white sky and prayed to a God I wasn't sure I believed in to heal the girl I loved.

9

I paced outside of the ER for the next hour. Two ambulances came through and a homeless guy with a cigarette dangling from his mouth shuffled out, asking if I had a light. I wanted to scream. He had no idea what his question did to the ball of hate inside me.

I stared too long at the electric glass door leading back to Ani, hoping any minute she might walk out. Would she even be able to walk? Someone had put a fucking lighter inside of her. The image burrowed in my brain. Had they tried to light it? I swallowed the bile in the back of my throat.

I wanted to kill someone. I'd never felt like that in my life before, but my fists clenched and unclenched, ready to beat the hell out of anyone I could get my hands on. Ani had been raped. And maybe was too drunk to remember. Was it more than one guy? My nails bit into my palms and I glared at the door.

Kate walked out. She looked like shit. I probably did too.

"They got it out. She's okay. I guess the damage wasn't too bad. She had to get a few stitches. But it's out."

I took a deep breath and leaned forward with my hands on my knees. After a minute, I looked up at Kate.

"Can I see her?"

"I told her you were here. She's worried about what you'll think of her. She's afraid to see you."

I slumped onto the ground. Kate came up behind me and put a hand on my shoulder.

"Beez, she doesn't remember much and she's blaming herself," Kate said. "The rape counselor is trying to help her, but you know how Ani can be."

"That's why I have to see her. Please, Kate."

Kate looked at me and shook her head. "I'll do my best. I can't promise anything. And the counselor told her she doesn't have to see you if she doesn't want to."

"Please." I couldn't leave without seeing her. I couldn't breathe completely until I knew she was okay.

Kate stood up and walked back into the ER. I didn't move. Ani was afraid to see me. *Me*. I stood frozen for a full minute, cool wind scraping my cheeks. Finally I sat on the curb like a kicked dog. I flipped my phone open to call my mom, but shut it again. Ani didn't even want her own mom involved with this, how could I tell mine?

Ten minutes later the doors slid open behind me.

"Okay, come on. She'll see you," Kate said.

I got up quickly and shook myself. I tried to relax my fists. The crumbling parts of me were being held together only by my determination to help Ani. I shut my eyes and focused on my goal. I followed Kate into the pale, dingy pink walls of the ER labyrinth. My shoes squeaked as I walked past doctors and nurses. The thin old woman from earlier sat in a wheelchair now, coughing constantly.

Ani was in a room at the end of the hall. Kate stood with her hand on the handle and searched my face. I inhaled and held my breath. Finally I nodded and she swung the door open.

I walked in and found Ani in a white-and-blue hospital gown, curled up sideways on the bed. She looked at me and her eyes filled with tears. I opened my mouth, but then shut it. I couldn't move.

"What are you doing here, Bumble?" Her voice cracked.

I did my best to half smile and stepped slowly forward. I reached the edge of her bed and pushed her hair behind her ear. I almost never saw her hair down and loose. I'd expected some bruises on her face or something, but she looked like the same Ani.

"I came for you. Baby, what happened?"

A strange woman wearing a Georgetown sweatshirt and jeans stepped forward and put her hand on Ani's shoulder. She pursed her lips and squinted at me.

"Ani's been through this with the police already."

Ani touched the woman's hand and adjusted her position in the bed so she was sitting up more. She winced and I pulled back slightly.

"It's okay, Beth. I don't mind," she said to the woman.

The counselor didn't even glance at me. She kept her gaze zeroed on Ani. "It's your right to have privacy."

Ani nodded. "I know. But Ben's safe. He can know everything." Her eyes shifted to me. "Beth's the counselor. She's been here the whole time."

"Why didn't you call me?" I asked. Ani focused on her hands twisting around the thin sheet covering her. God, I was such an asshole. "Forget I said that. Don't worry about it. I just want to help."

Ani lifted her eyes and tried to smile. It was pathetic and nothing like the beautiful smile she normally greeted me with. The room grew uncomfortably quiet. I shifted my weight from one foot to the other and tried to figure out what to say.

"I don't remember very much," Ani finally said.

"You were pretty wasted, huh?"

The counselor, Beth, stepped in front of me with her mouth

in a small frown. Her hands pressed together in front of her almost like she was going to pray. "Can I speak with you outside for a moment?"

Outside? What the hell was this woman's problem? I stepped forward and squeezed Ani's too-cold hand before following Beth out the door. She turned on me the moment we were out of Ani's earshot.

"Listen, I know that this is a really difficult time for you, but accusing Ani of drinking too much and asking her to rehash everything that happened is not helpful," she said through pinched lips. "We need to try to empower her, not blame her for her choices."

"What?" I said. She sounded like she was reading from a book. What did that even mean?

"You probably don't even realize it, and I understand you're in shock, but you made a victim-blaming statement and I think you need to be careful of what you say to Ani right now," she said more slowly, like English wasn't my first language.

"I'm not blaming her."

"Pointing out her alcohol consumption implies she was somehow at fault for what happened. Like she asked to be raped because she was drinking at a party. I'm sure that's not what you were trying to say, but you just need to be aware that your words mean a lot to her right now."

I kicked the wall. I kicked it again. So many emotions were

pouring through me and I couldn't stand this woman telling me I didn't know how to talk to my girlfriend.

"Jesus, lady, of course I wasn't saying she asked for it. All I asked was if she was wasted. That's my girlfriend in there, who just got out of some sort of surgery because a douche bag left a lighter in her after she'd made out with him. I'm doing the best I can here."

She took a step back. "Excuse me?"

"I am doing the best I can," I repeated in the same infuriating way she talked to me.

Her face softened and I thought I might start shaking I was so overwhelmed with everything. She took a step forward but didn't touch me.

"Ben, right?" she asked so quietly I barely heard her. I gave a tiny nod. "I'm sorry. This is a difficult time for everyone. Friends and family members often are grieving as much as victims are. I'm not trying to negate your feelings. But if you want to help Ani right now, you need to be open and supportive. I know how painful this must be for you, but we need to make this completely about helping Ani."

"Where did you learn to talk like that? I don't even understand what you're saying," I said.

"I'll give you some pamphlets and contact information for support groups of partners of survivors before I leave, but please think about what I'm saying. Ani's confused and overwhelmed right now; you don't need to add to that."

What could I say? Nothing she said made much sense, but she was probably right about Ani being overwhelmed. And it was clear that Beth thought I was being a selfish prick. Even though I'd only asked one question. But didn't I have a right to be? What the hell had gone down at that party?

I took several deep breaths. I needed to man up and forget what Kate had told me for a little while so I could be there for Ani.

"Yeah. Okay. I got it. Just give me a second here."

Beth nodded and pointed out the men's room at the end of the hall.

I walked numbly toward it and locked the door when I got inside. I slid to the ground and rubbed my eyes with my fists. Fuck. I banged my head against the door. Fuckfuckfuckfuck-fuck. I banged again and again. I rolled my neck on my shoulders and finally pulled myself off the floor.

10

Beth waited for me outside Ani's door. She didn't ask any questions, just gave my shoulder a small squeeze. So she was semi-human after all. She opened the door. We shuffled in and I tried again to relax my fisted hands. Ani was staring at the posters on the wall while Kate spoke in hushed tones on the phone in the corner. She hung up when I walked in and gave her a look, pointing to Ani.

Kate moved closer to the bed. "I told your mom Ben picked you up from my house this morning after the sleepover. She's pissed you aren't answering your cell. You're gonna have to call her soon."

Ani nodded but didn't say anything. I stepped forward and traced the line of her cheek. She flinched for a second, but then closed her eyes and leaned into my hand. The part of me that had felt so empty from the moment I got Kate's phone call started to fill with warmth.

"We'll get through this, baby," I said, and stroked her hair.

She looked up at me with her big eyes brimming with tears, and I sat down on the edge of the bed, afraid my legs would buckle under the weight of her sadness.

"I don't remember anything. I had two drinks, maybe three. They must have been really strong. I didn't eat that much beforehand so maybe it was that. Kate said I was saying crazy things, but I swear, I don't remember any of it."

I leaned into her and she clung to me, silent tears falling on my shirt. Hers and mine. I brushed them away and wrapped my arms around her as gently as I could.

Beth pulled out a binder she had with her and handed me a piece of paper, which I ignored and put on the small table next to Ani.

"There's a possibility that Ani was given date rape drugs."

My head whipped up. Beth pointed to the sheet on the table. I picked it up and looked at it: *GHB, Ketamine, and Rohypnol—What You Need to Know about Date Rape Drugs*.

"Date rape drugs? Like roofies?"

Beth nodded. "The doctors are doing a drug screen for them, but I should tell you drug screens frequently turn up negative, even if they have been used. Most date rape drugs don't last in the system very long, and since this happened to Ani last night, we may not find out for sure."

I glanced at the descriptions and effects of the various drugs. My body sagged in momentary relief. Roofies would explain a lot: her kissing some other guy, her talk about hooking up with all of them, her blackout, her inability to remember what happened.

Kate stepped toward me. "I don't think she got her own drinks but I'm not sure. The guys were bartending for a bunch of people. They might've made Ani's." Her voice dropped to a whisper. "I heard one of them say something to his friend like 'We're gonna love this ride' when he was going upstairs with her."

Puke coated the back of my throat. My eyes whipped around the room to focus on something other than Ani's devastated face. Her tree necklace hung from a knob on the side table drawer. I reached out to touch it, but Ani snatched it away and squeezed her hand around it. Her eyes shut tight and her head kept swiveling back and forth in denial.

I grabbed Kate's shoulder. "Why you didn't fucking think to stop them from taking her upstairs?"

Kate looked down, but Ani answered, reaching out for me and tugging me closer. "It wasn't her fault. They didn't drag me upstairs. People saw me go. Kate told me I went with them willingly. That I wouldn't listen to her. That I said I was going to . . ." Ani choked on the words and my stomach clenched. She took a deep breath. "It's not Kate's fault. Leave her alone."

Beth ignored the tension in the room and continued, "Whether date rape drugs were involved or not doesn't really change much. Ani still doesn't know the identity of the perpetrator."

"We can find out," I said, my mind already racing to ask Kate who she recognized from the party.

Beth stared at me for a beat and raised her eyebrows. I bit the inside of my cheek and nodded. She went on like she was reading from some sort of rape survivor script. "Although the police are investigating the party, chances are, they won't pursue it."

"What? Why the hell not?" I shifted my position and Ani winced. Beth frowned at me and I tried to relax.

"The police will look into it. They might ticket the parents of the kid whose house the party was at for contributing to underage drinking, although they tend to threaten that more than actually doing it. But if Ani doesn't want to testify about the sexual assault, then they'll abandon the rape kit and move on. Even if she does want to go forward, the state's attorney may not pursue it in court. Either way, it's their decision. They tend to go after things they can win and there are many unknowns in this case. I don't mean to sound negative, but this is the reality of the situation. Regardless, it is *Ani's* decision how she wants to proceed," she said, focusing on me.

I clamped down on my tongue and tasted blood. Ani laced her fingers in mine. I stared at her. I'd never seen her look so tiny before. Her chin trembled a little when her gaze met mine.

"It's over. I'm done." She sounded so broken. I squeezed her hand too tight, willing the pieces of her back together, trying to fuse them with mine. "I don't want them to pursue it. I need to go home."

11

"*I'm* taking Ani home," I whispered to Kate.

Beth was going over paperwork with Ani. Her voice droned on and I wondered if she'd done this hundreds of times before or if this was her first time and she'd memorized all the things to say from a book. Ani stared at the pamphlets before her, not even registering what Beth pointed to, and pulled at the sleeves of the hospital gown. She dropped her necklace onto the sheet next to her.

"I don't think that's the best idea," Kate whispered back.

"Why not? Her mom thinks she's with me."

"You're not exactly in the best shape to drive right now," she said, pointing to my clenched fists.

"Back off. She's my girlfriend, I'm taking her home. You've done enough."

"What's that supposed to mean?" she hissed. Her skin was

flushed and her usually straight black hair looked like a bird had nested in it.

I shook my head. "Nothing. It doesn't mean anything. I don't blame you for what happened. This is on me. I should've been there. I just . . . I want to take her home."

"Ben . . . ," Kate started, but I held a hand up. I looked toward Ani. She was staring at us, but she didn't seem to have heard anything we said.

"I'll take you home, baby," I said, and stepped closer to her. She shifted back slightly and a hole formed in my chest.

She slid off the opposite side of the bed and gathered her clothes to her chest. I pointed to her abandoned necklace. She picked it up and dropped it into the trash. I opened my mouth to say something, but the dagger eyes from Kate and Beth stopped me.

On the way home, I glanced at Ani every few minutes, but she wouldn't look at me; she stared out the window with her fingers moving up and down, tracing the patterns of the cross-walks we passed. Beth had given her sweatpants and a T-shirt from a bag she had with her. She said most rape survivors have their clothes taken for evidence so she always brought extra clothes to the ER. The clothes were way too big for her, and made Ani look much younger than seventeen.

"What are you going to tell your mom?" I asked to break the silence.

"Nothing." She didn't look at me. Her fingers continued to move up and down.

"What?" I swerved my Jeep to the side of the road. The car to my left honked and I laid on my horn in response. Ani touched my wrist, and my hands returned to gripping the steering wheel.

I pivoted and shifted her to face me. "Nothing? You're not going to tell your mom anything? Ani, she's gonna know something is wrong. Those aren't even your clothes."

"I'll tell her I barfed on my clothes last night and had to get some extra ones from Kate."

"What about for your follow-up appointment? The doctor said he wanted to make sure you were healing." I swallowed back bile as I said it and hoped Ani didn't notice the disgust on my face. Why would someone have chosen to leave a lighter in her?

She turned from me and leaned against the window. "I can go by myself anytime. The doctor and Beth said I didn't have to tell my mom. I can drop by the clinic connected to the hospital to have them check my stitches. There aren't even that many. It was a little tear."

I took her wrist and tugged her so she had to look at me. "But why wouldn't you tell her? You tell her everything. She could help."

She pulled her hand away from me and swiped at a few

tears forming in the corners of her eyes. "No. No way. She'd freak."

"Why would you say that?"

Ani bit her bottom lip. It was so dry and chapped, it bled a little. She swiped her hand over her mouth and the red streaked her thumb. She licked her lips and looked at her lap. "One time when I was six, my cousin masturbated in front of me and she went ape shit. She totally cut all ties with that side of my family and then she and I had to go to crappy family therapy for nine months."

I recoiled. "What? Wait, what happened?"

Ani shook her head. "It was stupid. My fourteen-year-old cousin locked me in the bathroom with him and then got off while I watched."

"God, Ani, I'm sorry. I don't . . ."

She placed her hand on mine. "The point is, my mom flipped about it and we had to go see this idiot psychologist who asked me a bunch of stupid questions and had me play with toys. Then Gayle pretty much hijacked the rest of the sessions, talking about what a shitty mom she was and how she couldn't do anything right. By the end, I spent most of every session trying to make her feel better about it all and she hadn't even been the one to see my cousin's dick. It sucked and I'm not going through it again."

"This is hardly a cousin masturbating," I argued. I blinked

away the image of a young Ani being forced to watch a guy jack off. It was too much. I couldn't handle it.

"Still, how do you imagine a conversation with my mom going? 'Hey, Gayle, I screwed around with an unknown number of guys at a party where I got drunk, danced like a slut, and announced to everyone within hearing distance that I was gonna hook up with all these dudes.' I'm sure she'll be super-proud of me after that. And she definitely wouldn't somehow turn it into another reason for a Gayle pity party. Ha. Pass."

I flinched and shook my head. "That's not how last night went."

"How do you know?" she practically yelled at me. "Were you there? Because I was and I don't remember any of it and Kate was, and apparently, that's exactly how it went."

"Someone probably slipped you a roofie. You heard what Beth said, it might not show up in your system, but it could still have happened. That wasn't really *you* doing all that stuff."

"Oh, really? Did someone else get a surgical procedure this morning to have a lighter taken out of her vagina? Because I gotta tell you, it sure felt like it was me."

I started to shake. I rolled down the window so some of the cold autumn breeze could get into the car. The air was thick and itchy on my skin. I couldn't concentrate. Pieces of the conversation from the hospital echoed in my head. I looked at the plastic bag that sat between our seats filled with pamphlets about STDs, rape trauma syndrome, date rape drugs, and a handful of morning-after pills Ani was supposed to take in twenty-four hours. Somewhere in the bag was Beth's organization's name and a crisis hotline phone number on a card. She'd pressed it into my hand as we were leaving and told me that both of us should reach out to someone when we were ready.

I leaned my head against the wheel and turned to Ani. "I'm sorry, baby. I should've been there. I'm so fucking sorry." It was the only thing I could choke out.

She was in my arms then, sobbing. Her anguish racked her body, and she clutched at me like I was the only thing keeping her above water. I squeezed my eyes shut so no tears would fall. I brushed my hand over the rough fabric of her T-shirt and pulled her more tightly into my lap.

"We'll get through this. I promise," I said, but I didn't really have the first idea how.

"I'm not telling my mom. I won't put her through that. Or me. I don't know what happened and I can't handle all the questions. You have to promise not to tell her anything. Promise, Beez."

I hushed her and ran my hand through her hair. "I promise. We'll work through this together. I'll help you. You won't be alone."

She stretched to kiss me and my body instinctively deepened

the kiss. She didn't move her mouth and her chapped lips didn't open. I pulled back.

"Sorry. I didn't mean . . . I don't want to hurt you."

She shook her head and wiped her hand across her mouth. "It's not you. I just can't stop thinking of the stuff the doctor said and all those questions the police asked."

I rubbed my finger across the speck of blood on her bottom lip and lifted her back into her seat. I fastened the seat belt around her and she leaned back and closed her eyes.

"We'll get through this," I said again as I put the Jeep into drive and headed back down the road to her place.

I walked her to her door, my arm wrapped tightly around her.

Gayle had it open before Ani had even put the key in the lock.

"You're in big trouble," she said, staring hard at Ani.

I opened my mouth, but Ani pressed her hand against my shoulder.

"I know," she answered. "I'm sorry. I drank too much."

Gayle released a breath. "Obviously. You look terrible. Why didn't you call me? You know better than to get drunk at a party. What were you thinking?"

I bit my tongue against the words itching to come out and focused on Ani's face.

"Sorry, Mom," Ani said again, and walked slowly into her

living room, her bag filled with Beth's pamphlets tucked away in her backpack.

I stood in the doorway, trying to figure out what to say. Ani's eyes pleaded with me, tightening the muzzle of my promise to stay silent.

"And you," Gayle said, swiveling back to me. "You should have dropped her off as soon as you picked her up from Kate's. At the very least, you should have called me. It was irresponsible, Ben. She was in no condition to go on an outing with you."

I nodded and accepted the reprimand without argument. I deserved her accusations of irresponsibility. I deserved much more. My muscles tightened. I felt like I was being held underwater, pushing up against something that kept pressing me farther down. Short breaths barely escaped my lungs.

"I'm sorry," I said, and turned to Ani. "I'm sorry, Ani. I should have taken better care of you." My voice cracked.

Ani nodded and I moved to leave.

"Thanks for bringing me home," she called out softly.

The door clicked behind me and I flinched when I heard Gayle's stinging voice say, "You're grounded. Four weeks. No parties. No dates. No picnics with Ben. You're here or you're at school. No exceptions."

I couldn't hear Ani's mumbled reply, but I knew she wouldn't argue.

I got in my car and drove to the pool. Weekend lap swim. Open to the public. My feet slapped against the locker room floor, leading me to a back corner where I couldn't be seen. I fumbled from my clothes and pulled on a pair of trunks I always kept in my car. No goggles, but it didn't matter. My eyes stung already from the pressure of tears. I plunged into an empty lane of the pool and swam until I could barely lift my arms anymore. No steady rhythm, more a driving force that pushed me past feeling. I barely took breaths, just pumped and kicked and swam more.

When every muscle shook in pain, I dragged myself out of the water and sat on the edge staring at the T-shaped lines on the bottom for what might have been hours. Huddled back in the corner of the locker room, I texted Ani but she didn't answer. Everything hurt and I didn't know what to do to make it better. So I drove home and went to bed without speaking to anyone.

12

Ani didn't show up for school on Monday. My phone pinged as I choked down frozen waffles and ignored Michael's humming at the breakfast table.

I'm not ready to face school yet. My mom called in sick for me.

I texted back: *I'll be w/ u the whole time.*

I know. I need a few more days.

I replied: *I love you.*

Me too.

I stared at the screen until my eyes watered. Michael finally thumped me on the back and dragged me to the car, whining about needing to get to school early.

I parked the Jeep two blocks from school and walked slowly to the entrance, stepping on the laces of the shoes I hadn't bothered to tie. There were people everywhere. Too-loud talking and too much touching. Everyone seemed to be touching each other. I couldn't stop looking at hands. I couldn't escape them. I wanted to crawl inside myself and disappear.

I moved numbly to my classes, ignoring the people around me. By ten o'clock that morning, I was glad Ani didn't make it in.

My head ached from staring too long at the fluorescent lights. I stumbled as I reached my locker before English. I leaned over to tie my shoe and heard it.

"Firecrotch."

The voice came from behind me, not meant for my ears, but paralyzing me all the same.

I moved quickly, eating up the distance between me and the two junior guys who'd been talking.

"What? What did you say?"

"Dude, chill."

"No. What did you say?" Blood pumped violently through me.

"We were just talking about some chick at a party."

My elbow slammed him into a locker. "What. Did. You. Say?"

His bugged-out, panicky eyes glanced behind me to his friend. "I was talking about a chick who got off in front of a bunch of guys at a party. She fucked a lighter so everyone's calling her Firecrotch."

My body flooded with anger. I shook my head. This wasn't

happening. How did people know already? My heart beat so loud I barely registered the guys' voices. The one behind me pulled me back. He grabbed his friend and they mumbled to each other. Finally one of them looked me over and shook his head sadly.

"She's yours, huh? Sorry, man. That sucks."

I pushed my way out of the building and started walking toward the track. *She fucked a lighter.* No. No. She couldn't have. Even if someone gave her roofies. Even if she did a table dance. Even if she did say she was going to get with a bunch of guys. Pressure built in my lungs. My throat was clogged with anger and disgust and a wad of sadness I couldn't breathe past. Everything blurred.

"Beez," a voice called, but I ignored it and walked faster.

Running footsteps caught up to me and I finally turned. I wanted to beat the hell out of someone. Kate stepped back when she saw my face.

"You've heard what people are saying," she said.

I nodded and shoved my hands into my pockets.

"I didn't tell anyone."

I nodded again.

"But you know there were a lot of people at that party. . . ."

I held up my hand. I closed my eyes and forced myself to ask the question I'd been worrying over since I'd dropped Ani off from the hospital. "How many guys? How many do you think there were?"

Kate shook her head and took a half step back. "I don't know. She went upstairs with maybe twelve people, girls and guys, but some of them came back down. Some of them could have gone into other rooms. It was a pretty big house."

I grabbed Kate's shoulders and squeezed. "Who else saw her? Who would know what happened?"

She looked at my hands. "There weren't that many people from our school there. It was a big party, but I only recognized maybe twenty people."

I dropped my hands and stepped away from her. "Well, someone from this school knows what happened because guys I've never even talked to before are calling her Firecrotch and saying she fucked a lighter. And Ani sure as hell doesn't remember anything." I kicked at the grass and a clump unleashed itself from the ground. I kicked again. "Please," I pleaded to Kate. "I have to know what happened."

"Why? You heard what that counselor said. It's not going to do Ani any good. She's not going to get back her memory if she was passed out at the time. She doesn't want to testify against the guy or guys or whatever. And what if it's worse than we think? What if they used other things with her?"

I squeezed my eyes tight against the image of guys searching for different things to put inside of Ani. I wanted to puke.

104

Kate put her hand on my shoulder. "Or what if what they're saying is true? What if Ani asked them to?"

I flinched and fisted my hands. "No one fucking asks for that. Don't even start with that shit."

Kate pushed her hair back and searched my face.

"What? Just say it," I barked at her. I wanted everything out on the table. Kate knew more than I did and I had to have as many facts as I could if I was going to help Ani.

She wavered for a second but then nodded. "You didn't see her. She was acting like a complete slut. A lot of people heard her say she was going to hook up with all those guys. She didn't tell just me."

She couldn't have hit me harder. I bent over and grabbed my knees. Ani wasn't a slut. She was direct. I couldn't have read her wrong all this time. My hands shook. I had to get out of there. I couldn't listen to Kate anymore. I turned my back on her and walked toward the bleachers alongside the track. This time she didn't follow me.

How drunk would Ani have had to be to say that stuff? Was hooking up with a bunch of guys her intention when she went with all of them upstairs? I thought about the pamphlet Beth had given me about date rape drugs. I'd looked up more information online about them when I'd gotten up this morning, but there were so many different kinds of drugs out there. Ani seemed to have had some of the effects of the drugs, but she could've just had too much to drink. I'd seen Ani drunk before and she didn't get all slutty, but I knew enough girls who did to think it might be possible.

My brain was flooded with questions and doubt. How the hell were we going to get past this without either of us knowing anything?

I went to see Ani after school. I texted Kevin and told him to make an excuse to Coach for me. He texted back: *What the hell is going on?* I ignored him.

"We're not talking about the rape," Ani said when she opened the door.

"Okay," I said without hesitation. Beth had told me to try and empower her as much as I could; let her steer the conversation, give her choices in everything. "But are you feeling okay?"

She nodded and pulled me into her room. The shades were drawn and her bed was a rumpled mess of covers. She'd added two or three more blankets on top of her quilt. The clothes she'd worn home from the hospital were in a pile on the floor by her bed.

"Were you cold?" I asked, pointing to the blanket pile.

She shook her head. "Building a nest. Want to get in with me?"

I half smiled for the first time all day. Ani was still here. We were together. We could get through it. I slipped off my shoes and hooded sweatshirt before climbing into her bed with her. I wrapped my arms around her and tucked her head beneath my chin. The scent of her made me dizzy. I inhaled and exhaled three times, drawing full breaths into my lungs, soothing the numbness I'd felt since hearing the guys in the hall. Ani's body didn't relax so I started to trace circles on her back. She sat up and straddled my waist. She pulled her shirt over her head and her braless nipples immediately reacted to the cold.

"What are you doing?" I said, and stopped her hands tugging at my shirt. "What are you *doing*?"

"I thought you might fuck me."

I shot up and grabbed her shirt from next to me.

"What?" I tried to pull the shirt over her head, but she ducked away and stood up. Everything went still in the room. We stared at each other. Ani put her hands on her hips, her naked chest rising and falling with her breath.

"I. Want. You. To. Fuck. Me."

"Are you crazy, Ani? We can't have sex. You have stitches. And even if we could, don't you want to take this slowly? Sort of ease into it when you're more ready."

She snatched her shirt from me and held it over her chest. "No," she said through gritted teeth, "I don't want to ease into it. I don't want to fucking ease into it."

"Ani." My eyes started to burn again. "Ani. Please."

"Ben," she said breathlessly, and dropped her shirt to the

ground. "I need you to fuck me. I want to close my eyes tonight and think that the last guy who was inside of me cared about me and maybe even loved me a little, instead of thinking the last guy inside of me thought I was so worthless he left a lighter as a parting gift."

I recoiled at her words and dragged my hands across my face. "Jesus, Ani, stop saying that. Stop reminding me. Don't you think I want you to forget all that too? I wish I could touch you and make it go away, put my hands on you so you'd only think about me. But this isn't the way. You're not ready for this."

She collapsed onto the bed and started crying noiselessly. She curled herself into a tiny ball. I wrapped my arms around her and tried to soothe her, but she wouldn't relax. She shivered and pulled her knees tighter to her chest.

I wanted to ask her so many things. But she wouldn't know the answers. She was as lost as I was. More lost, really. My fingers worked over the knots in her hair.

"Will you come to school tomorrow?" I finally asked.

"I don't want to," she said, her voice barely a whisper, "but I think my mom will make me. She's already pissed about today. She thinks I skipped school because I'm still hungover from Saturday."

"Do you think maybe . . . ?" I started, but she got out of the bed before I could finish. She snatched her shirt up and tugged it on.

108

"No. No one is going to know about this. No one." Her eyes flashed and she crossed her arms over her stomach. "I'm not going to be *that* girl, the one everyone feels sorry for. The one everyone talks about."

I reached for her but she stepped back. "Okay," I said, and released a deep breath. "Whatever you want. Please, just come sit back down."

I couldn't tell her what I really thought. She seemed so fragile, I didn't think she could take the truth. But by now, the entire school had probably heard all the rumors. "Firecrotch" would move through the school like a twisted game of Telephone. Ani wasn't going to leave a party with a lighter inside of her and not have anyone know about it. I bit my tongue and reached for her again. She allowed me to take her hand and moved a step toward me. I willed my face to go blank. I didn't know how to warn her that she already was *that* girl.

I slowly drew her back down beside me. She curled into me again and I rubbed my hand along her arm. I pretended not to notice her shaking.

13

Ani came back to school on Wednesday. She'd bought herself an extra day somehow with Gayle but couldn't put things off any longer. I waited for her by the front entrance. Her mom dropped her off two minutes before the first bell rang, so I didn't have any time to talk to her. It was unusually warm but still she wore a coat over a hooded sweatshirt and jeans, like she was hiking through the woods and worried about ticks.

I took her hand as we walked into school and she let me. We hadn't walked more than fifteen feet toward her locker when Ani suddenly stilled. She glanced at people on both sides of the hallway, then slowly turned to face me. Her mouth pursed and she released my hand.

"They know? Did you say something?" she hissed.

"No."

"But they know?"

I nodded and tried to read the emotions crossing her face. The only one I recognized for sure was fear. I tried to wrap my arms around her, but she stepped back from me.

"You could have told me. I would have been more prepared."

I opened my mouth to answer but was interrupted by Morgan and her posse of girlfriends.

"Hey, Firecrotch, do you need to borrow a lighter?" Morgan stood in front of us with her arms crossed and a smirk on her face.

"You cunt." I took a step to go after her, but Ani put her hand on my shoulder and shook her head. Morgan lifted her eyebrows and turned away, whispering something I couldn't hear to her bitchy friends. The other girls giggled.

"Do you want to get out of here?" I said to Ani in a low voice, the echo of mean-girl laughter ringing in my ears.

"Where would I go? My mom's not going to let me skip school."

I tried to take her hand again, but she loosened her grip and wrapped her arms around herself. Almost like she was hugging herself, a little kid keeping monsters away. It tore through me. Sliced at my insides until the food I'd forced down from breakfast threatened to hurl out of me.

"What are they saying, Ben? Tell me what you've heard. Everything."

I closed my eyes and shook my head.

"I'm gonna find out anyway. What am I in for? Tell me."

I pulled her to the side of the hallway and glanced around to make sure no one could hear us. Every pair of eyes that passed flicked over Ani in derision or pity. I cupped her face in my hands and was glad she didn't pull away this time.

"Listen, I love you and I know you're going to get past this. It doesn't matter what they're saying. I'll go up against all these bitches if you want me to."

"Tell me." Her voice sounded hard.

I let out a deep breath. "They're saying you got off with a lighter in front of a bunch of guys."

Ani reared back. I pulled her into an embrace, but she stood frozen like a board. I ran my fingers along her shoulders, trying to knead out the tension. Her arms stayed at her sides, her fingers curling into the sleeves of her sweatshirt.

A guy in a basketball shirt moved closer to us. "Hey, Fire-crotch, when's your next show scheduled?"

Ani started to shake and I pushed her to the side to get my hands on the guy. I slammed him against a locker and started to pummel him. My fists kept finding places to attack. His blood covered my hands and shirt but I didn't care. He might have hit me back, but I didn't feel anything except relief at finally releasing my anger. *Pound. Harder. Pound.*

I heard Ani's voice scream at me to stop, but it was a far-away plea, nothing like the immediacy of hearing cartilage crunch beneath my knuckles. I couldn't stop, it felt too good. From the corner of my eye, I saw Ani slump to the floor, hugging her legs tightly and burying her face in her knees. My hands hurt, but I kept swinging until someone pulled me off the guy. He was moaning and I tried to kick him one more time, but I was too far away. I gathered saliva in my mouth and spit on him.

A driver's ed teacher escorted me to the main office, where I sat motionless as the guidance counselor talked at me. I said nothing, just stared at my bloody hands opening and closing, wishing for another fight.

They gave me a three-day suspension for fighting on school grounds. When my mom picked me up, she didn't say a word to me. She had a brief conversation with the guidance counselor and pointed me to the door.

"What happened, Ben?" she demanded the minute I got in the car.

"My Jeep's in the lot. I can drive home."

"No. Your father can get it tonight. What happened?"

"Nothing," I said, buckling myself in and mentally preparing for her lecture. I glanced at the windows on the first floor of the school and was suddenly struck by what I'd done. Shit. Ani was on her own. Alone in a den of vipers. Shit. Shit. Shit.

"No way, mister. You got a three-day suspension for fighting and I want to know why. So let's hear it." Mom's hair had fallen loose from her bun and she looked exhausted. She was working too hard, staying up too late studying for grad school. She didn't need this.

"I don't have anything to say. It was a mistake." It had been. I wasn't exactly sorry for it, but I hated the thought of Ani watching me lose my shit. I hated that my mom had to come get me.

"You're absolutely right it was a mistake, but this isn't like you. You've never been in trouble for fighting. Did that kid do something to provoke you?"

"Mom," I said, and turned to her, "remember how you're always saying that we need to respect one another?" She nodded. "I need you to do that now. I'd like you to let this go. It was a mistake. It won't happen again. But I don't want to talk about it. Please." I would not make this her problem. I couldn't. And I didn't have any more words to give her that wouldn't break my promise to Ani.

Her lips pursed in a tight line as she searched my face. Her hand grazed over a cut I'd gotten above my eye. Finally she released a breath and put the key in the ignition.

"You're grounded for six weeks. I'll assume this was some sort of lapse with you, and we'll leave it alone as long as this is the last time that I'm called from work to pick you up. Clear?"

I nodded and stared at the windows of school. I squeezed

my eyes shut and tried to shake off the image of Ani screaming at me and hiding her face in her knees while she watched me beat some kid to a pulp on the hallway floor.

I got home and completely lost my shit the minute I saw the picture on my desk of Ani and me at my swim meet, the pink bumblebee poster clutched in her hand. I tore my room apart. I pulled the swirly, colorful star painting Ani had made me from the wall and ripped papers from my bulletin board. I kicked my laundry basket so many times my toe hurt. I kept hearing the guy asking Ani about her next show. The echo of bitchy girl laughter was like a soundtrack playing over and over again in my head. I finally collapsed on my bed, shaking so hard I could barely pull my shoes off.

I'd left Ani at the mercy of school gossip for three days. She wasn't going to have me to protect her. What the hell had I been thinking? I had to make it right. I searched beneath shredded homework and too many swim T-shirts for my cell phone. I found it, hoping for a message from Ani, but it was blank. I flipped it open and tried to call, but she didn't answer. I hit my head against my bedpost and tried again. Nothing. I called Kate.

"I screwed up," I started.

"Yeah, I heard."

"You've got to look out for Ani."

"No shit, but you should be doing it too. That shit you

pulled was completely selfish. You're not doing Ani any favors by fighting."

"I couldn't help it. You should have heard what that prick said," I practically yelled, pissed at myself because she was right.

"It doesn't matter. I don't care what he said and neither should you. We're supposed to be supporting Ani. Do you see this as helping?"

I inhaled a big gulp of air. "Of course not. I know. I fucked up. Sorry. Can you tell her I'm sorry?"

"You should tell her," Kate said in a clipped tone that was starting to get annoying.

"She's not answering her phone. I'll tell her, but if you see her, could you just tell her I won't do anything like that again?"

"Fine. But I think you should call that counselor Beth. Maybe she could help you figure some stuff out?"

"Fuck you, Kate. I'm fine."

"Whatever. Tell that to the kid with the broken face."

She clicked off and I stared at the ceiling of my bedroom. Pale gray like the sky above the lake. I focused on the point above my head so long, spots started to blur my vision.

I was in hell. I had to figure out how to apologize to Ani and make sure she was okay. I texted her and called her again. I cleaned my room and then sent her an e-mail. No response.

Dad came home and dropped my keys onto my desk. His

dress shirtsleeves were rolled up, but the rest of him looked as pressed and polished as always. My gaze moved from him to the triangular stone key ring. Ani had thrown away her necklace at the hospital. Tossed it like it meant nothing to her. Why?

"Would you like to discuss it?" Dad's voice hitched, tight with an emotion I didn't understand.

"No."

"You know better than this."

Eyes back to the key ring, I bit my tongue and nodded at Dad.

"Your mother talked to you about your punishment."

I nodded again and he released a long breath.

"We talk to our family."

"Sometimes," I said. "But sometimes we need to figure out things for ourselves."

He pushed his hands into his pockets. "Yes. Sometimes we do. But are you sure this is one of those times?"

I leaned back on my bed and looked at the ceiling again. His disapproval rolled over me in waves. I glanced toward Ani's picture on the wall, then back to the key ring, and finally to my dad. "Yes. I'm sure."

He sighed and left the room.

I checked my e-mail and phone again. And again. Nothing. Ani was radio silent.

14

When my three-day suspension was over, I returned to school early to swim. Nothing seemed to work right in the water. My times were slow, I felt like I was pulling my arms through sludge. Coach read me the riot act about losing those days of practice, and then told me I had better keep myself clean if I wanted to get the scholarship at Iowa. I took a quick shower and went to find Ani before homeroom. Halfway down the hall, I saw her in front of her locker, scrubbing the outside of the door. I took a few steps toward her but felt an arm tug me into the alcove by the water fountain.

"Leave her be," Kate whispered.

I glanced at Ani, then back to Kate. "What's she doing?"

"Scrubbing her locker. Someone wrote 'FIRECROTCH'

on it in permanent ink. She doesn't want you to see," Kate answered in a low voice.

"Why the hell not?"

"She's worried you'll freak out again."

I swallowed the guilt gnawing at me and rolled my shoulders. "I'll be fine. I won't freak out."

"She asked me to make sure you didn't see her. This is humiliating enough for her as is."

I peeked my head out of the alcove and watched Ani brush away angry tears. I felt like I was being gutted. "So I'm just supposed to sit here and let her take care of this on her own."

"Yes," Kate said. "Come find her later. Don't make this any harder on her."

"That's totally ridiculous."

Kate pointed down the hall in the other direction and shooed me away. I took a step toward Ani. It was a compulsion. I could *not* let her deal with this on her own.

"Use some common sense. She doesn't want you to see this. You'll only make it worse," she hissed at me, and gave me the stink eye.

"Ridiculous," I mumbled again, and watched Ani brush away more tears. I stared at Kate, drew in a big breath, and stalked off in the opposite direction. What the hell kind of boyfriend could I be if Ani wouldn't let me help her?

After second period, I searched her out. She looked like shit, like she hadn't been sleeping and hadn't brushed her hair for the entire time I was gone. Her eyes were still red from crying earlier. She barely nodded at me when she saw me standing at her locker. The writing hadn't come off but had been blacked out with marker. I pretended not to notice it.

"Hey, how come you didn't call me back?" I asked as soon as she got close enough to hear me.

She shrugged and started to spin the combination on her locker.

"Well, are you okay?"

She looked up at me and raised her eyebrows.

"You know what I mean. Did anyone else give you a hard time?" People stared at us as they passed in the hallway. I wanted to lash out at all of them. Scream at their stupidity, their horrible backstabbing judgment. The blacked-out word made me feel like they were just as bad as the fucker who'd raped her in the first place.

Would Ani even mention it? At the very least, I could ask a janitor to paint over it. Then she wouldn't know I was involved. But Christ, why couldn't I be involved?

"Why do you care?" she said, finally breaking her silence. "Are you looking for more drama? To add more fuel to the rumors about me?"

"I was trying to defend you—" I started to explain.

"Don't bother," she interrupted.

I watched two guys pass and check out Ani from behind. My fists tightened but I didn't move. I took a deep breath and exhaled through my mouth. At this rate, I wasn't going to make it through the week without another fight.

"Did you look through that stuff Beth gave you?" I asked, trying to release the tightness in my shoulders.

I'd started reading stuff on the Internet about rape victims during my suspension. It had gotten to be too much after a while, but I'd read enough to know that Ani needed to talk to someone.

"The drug screen was negative," she said, and shoved a book into her backpack. "No date rape drugs. Just me table dancing and announcing my sluttyness to the room."

"A negative screen doesn't mean anything."

Tears coated the tip of her eyelashes, and she pressed her palms into her eyes. "Still a negative screen, though."

I nodded, trying not to show any emotion. A positive drug screen would have made everything so much easier. And it would have squelched the doubt that had been sitting in my gut since Kate first told me what had happened. But Beth had said date rape drugs disappeared from the body fairly quickly, so negative drug screens were common. It sucked not knowing for sure, but I held on to what Beth said and tried to push past the uncertainty in my mind.

"Do you need me to carry that?" I asked, pointing to her backpack.

"I'm not an invalid," she snapped. Then her eyes softened. "Sorry. I don't mean to yell at you. None of this is your fault."

I didn't say anything but turned to walk her to her next class. It *was* my fault. We both knew it. Nothing would have happened if I'd been at that party. A part of me wished she'd say it out loud. I deserved her venom. I'd left her to be raped, and even if she refused to blame me, her silence condemned me.

Kevin called out to me outside of fourth-period gym class. He approached slowly. He'd been trying to get a hold of me for a few days, but I'd avoided him. His face was full of pity when he reached me. I flinched. Was this how everyone was going to be with me now?

"What do you want?" I asked when he stood in front of me with his hands pressed together.

"I heard what happened."

"Did you hear from Kate or one of the assholes who're saying she fucked a lighter?"

He looked down. "Them first, but then I asked Kate what really happened because I didn't believe it."

"Everyone still talking about it?"

He shrugged. "I guess. It'll blow over eventually."

I clenched my jaw. Yeah, it'd blow over with them, but what

about Ani? Was she going to be left an angry shell of a girl?

"What did she tell her mom?" Kevin asked. He slid his foot halfway out of his untied shoe and shoved it back in.

"Nothing. She doesn't want to say anything."

"You don't think she'll find out? Won't she get hospital bills or whatever?" Kevin looked at me in surprise. I understood, I couldn't believe Ani would keep Gayle from all of it either, but she'd been determined not to tell her. I hoped it wouldn't last. Ani needed help.

"No hospital bills. This rape counselor said the state covers hospital costs for rape victims. It's some sort of law. Plus, it was county, so you know . . . and I guess Ani's old enough not to have needed a parent in the hospital with her. Even when they did the procedure." It sounded cold and medical and nothing like what'd really happened, but I didn't know how else to talk about it.

"That's messed up," Kevin said. "She should tell her mom."

I nodded. "What's everyone around here saying? Is it just the lighter thing?"

"Yeah, pretty much. I heard some other seniors say she stood on a table and announced to the party she was going to hook up with a bunch of guys, but then someone else said that was a lie. No one seems to have seen anything else. I don't think anyone from school was in the room when it happened or whatever."

In the room where she'd maybe gotten off with a lighter. In the room where she'd probably passed out and some prick decided he should have sex with her and leave a present inside her.

I pressed my eyes shut so tight splotches of light colored my vision when I finally opened them.

"Okay. Thanks for telling me, I guess. Do you think you could find out who was there? Not in the room, but at the party." I needed to let it go, but I couldn't. Someone had to have seen something more. Someone had to have been there for some of it.

"Yeah, I'll ask around."

"Thanks, man." I held out my hand and he bumped it.

"No problem. I'm sorry, Beez. This whole thing sucks."

It did suck. It more than sucked. It attacked me from the inside like a parasite. Every person I passed in the hall became someone who maybe knew something. Every time someone said, "What's up?" I searched their faces for a deeper meaning. I was becoming a lunatic.

I found Ani at lunchtime, sitting with Kate. The cafeteria was packed because it'd gotten too cold to sit outside. Tables full, bodies pressed together, loud voices and crappy melted-cheese smell wafted over everything. The usual swarm of normalcy. And somehow it all felt wrong. Out of sync and plastic.

"How's it going?" I asked, sliding onto the bench next to Ani. She stiffened and moved slightly away.

"Fine," she answered, staring at her untouched food.

"Classes okay?" I looked at Kate, who shook her head slightly.

Ani shrugged and rolled her sandwich bread into half a dozen little balls. My gaze landed on her neck.

"How come you don't wear your necklaces anymore?"

Her hand moved to her throat. "Turns out it was all bullshit. The stuff about us being connected. We're not. We're all on our own."

On our own. Of course she'd think that. I hadn't given her a reason to believe otherwise. Neither had Kate, honestly.

I put my hand on her knee and nudged her gently. "Things will get better."

She slid her knee from underneath my hand. I ignored her frostiness and moved an inch closer to her. She leaned farther away. It was like approaching a skittish dog. I released a breath and turned back to my lunch.

She lined up her chips and rolled the sandwich balls over them. Then she wadded everything together and tossed it in the trash. Every movement seemed so deliberate. Like she was somehow reminding her body how to do normal things. She stood to leave. I didn't know if I should follow, but she turned back to me suddenly.

"Are you coming?"

I took one large bite from my sandwich, tossed the rest, and followed Ani out of the cafeteria. Kevin caught my eye as I was leaving. He pointed to Ani in question. I shook my head and moved closer behind her, pretending that hundreds of eyes weren't watching us as we walked out.

She guided me to the slatted benches in the front entrance hallway. She pulled me down next to her and took one of my hands between both of hers.

"Don't say anything, okay?"

I nodded and she squeezed my hand tighter.

"I just want to sit with you for a while without having to say anything."

I shifted closer to her so that our hips were touching, and this time, she didn't draw away. Silence. Comfortable silence. Like how we were. A long breath of relief escaped my lungs.

Then the bell rang.

"Beez," a voice yelled from down the hall. A sea of faces poured out of the cafeteria. "You better wear a condom. You don't know what kind of diseases your little cum Dumpster is carrying around."

Ani gasped, dropped my hand, and stood up. Her body shook. I thought she might tear down the hall and beat the shit out of someone, but instead she crumpled onto the bench.

I didn't know whether to go after the douche bag who'd

torn apart the first moment of peace we'd had in days or to hold Ani so tight she'd forget what he said. In the end, she made the decision for me. She crept into my lap like a little girl and wrapped her fingers into my shirt, unwilling to let go.

I drove her home and she kissed me goodbye, but it was a weird kiss, sort of desperate and empty at the same time. She didn't ask me to come in, but I thought maybe it was because we were both grounded and I needed to get back for swim practice. I hoped she wasn't worried about me saying anything to her mom. Ani had asked me not to say anything to anyone, and I was going to keep my promise to her even if I wasn't sure it was the best choice. It was the only thing I could do.

15

Our life became a routine. I followed Ani from class to class, shielding her from the whispers and stares. At lunch she played with her food and then left before the period was over. I drove her home after school and raced back to get to practice on time.

"Your times are down, Baptiste," Coach said to me one day after practice.

"I know." I looked past him at the championship banners on the wall. Giant blue-and-gold triangles announcing every year we'd won state. The felt numbers of the past three years taunted me. But it was better than the disappointment on Coach's face.

"You're not in the pool enough," he said.

"There's a lot going on right now." I finally met his eyes. They were filled with concern. I grabbed the back of my neck and squeezed the tight muscles. Muscles that never relaxed anymore, even when I was swimming.

"'A lot going on' is not a good excuse. Your swimming needs to come first if you want that scholarship." His face was still red from screaming at us for ninety minutes, but his voice was low and understanding. "This isn't club anymore. We're in the real season, and every minute in the pool counts."

"I know."

"Do you want to talk about it?"

"No." My voice sounded raw. Brittle from all the energy it required to make it through every day with Ani.

"Fine. But it's an open offer. I'm here if you need me."

"Thanks."

I walked toward the showers and turned one on so hot I had difficulty breathing. My skin burned but I stayed beneath it for as long as I could, pushing everything from my mind but the physical sensation of scalding heat.

"I was thinking you should practice stick shift again," I said to Ani as I walked her to math class the next day.

I'd been steering her toward alternate routes, back stairways and low-traffic hallways, to avoid as many people as possible on the way to class. Ani made me cut it out after I'd gotten three tardy slips, so now we were in the middle of a busy corridor.

"We're still grounded," Ani answered. Her shoulders were

scrunched up and I wanted to touch them to make her relax, but I wasn't sure how she'd take it.

"I know. But after. I thought it'd be good for you to try again so we could be ready for the summer road trip."

Ani stopped and stared at me. No bubbly excitement about camping. No talk of the *Christmas Story* house. No promises of all the places we'd explore together. Just skepticism and distrust. She was going to call the whole thing off. Crap. The rape was going to ruin this, too.

Before she could say anything, I held my hand up. "It's too soon to talk about," I said. "I get it. But I'm not letting go of the chance that we might go still. A lot can happen between now and then." I hated the pleading in my voice. But I hated the idea that she was going to throw away all our plans, too. Like she refused to believe things would get better.

"Look out! Ani's coming! Fire in the hole! Take cover! Fire in the hole!" The voice came from the end of the hall. I whipped around to see who had shouted it, but my eyes couldn't zero in on anything other than the mass of people laughing around us.

I took a step, but then heard the slamming of books on the floor beside me. Ani had dropped her things and stood with her arms out. The venom in her eyes made me flinch.

"Fuck off!" she screamed. Her body swiveled to all the people around us. "Fuck off, all of you. I fucking hate every single one of you assholes."

I put my hand on her arm and she snatched it back. The entire hallway was silent for ten seconds before someone started whispering. Then louder talking. Then movement all around us. No one said anything to her or me. No one gave a shit.

Ani grabbed her books from the floor and sank down next to a glass case full of trophies. I moved next to her and tried to take her hand, but she pulled away again. She started dragging her fingernails down her wrists, leaving angry red scratches.

I pulled her hands away and refused to let go. She fisted them and struggled against me, but I wouldn't release her.

"Calm down."

"No. Fucking let me go, Ben. Now."

"No. Calm down. Take a deep breath."

She relaxed her hands and I loosened my grip, only to have her snatch them away and punch me on my chest. It didn't hurt. She punched me over and over until she fell into a heap in my lap. She started to sob and it took everything in me to hold back my own tears. People walked around us, staring, stepping over us, talking as if we couldn't hear them. Finally Ani pulled away and looked at her wrists.

"I'm so angry. I've never felt so angry before. Like I could hurt someone. Like it would feel so much better to pour everything inside of me out onto someone else. That's why you went after that guy, isn't it?"

I nodded and traced the red scratches along her forearms. "I don't want you to hurt yourself, baby."

Her fingers followed mine, trying to cover up the redness.

"Did you hear me, Ani? I don't want you to hurt yourself. I can't worry about that, too."

She slid her hand over my stubbly head. "I heard you. I won't hurt myself."

I hugged her and was relieved when she hugged me back, even if I could still feel all the knots in her shoulders.

It took about two more weeks for the whispering to die down. Ani and I were both still grounded, but things at school seemed to get a little less intense. Kevin found out a few names of guys who'd been at the party, but they couldn't really tell me anything. They'd seen Ani there. They'd heard her say she was going to hook up with the guys. They'd seen her dance on the kitchen table. They thought she was drunk and ignored her. They didn't know who she disappeared with or what happened to her. They looked at me with sympathy and I nearly beat the crap out of all of them.

"So I guess I fucked four guys at that party," Ani said one day at lunch while peeling the cheese off her sandwich.

I coughed on the lump of food in my mouth. "What? How do you know?"

"This girl in my gym class told me. She has a cousin who

goes to Morton. The guys I hooked up with must go there. She said that all of Morton is talking about the train ride. They're calling me the Manhole."

I squeezed my eyes shut and dug my nails into my palms. Why wasn't this going away?

"I guess it's better than Firecrotch," she continued without any expression on her face.

I met Kate's eyes across the table and we both cringed. Kate raised her eyebrows. So this was on me to fix. I took Ani's hand. She didn't seem to notice. I squeezed but she didn't even turn toward me. She just stared at her uneaten lunch.

"What girl told you this?"

Ani shrugged and didn't say anything.

"She could've been making it up. No one seems to really know anything about what happened," I said.

"Yeah, she could've been. But probably not. I mean, why would she? It sounds about right."

My stomach knotted and I took several deep breaths. Kate signaled me again with a tilt of her head.

"Ani," I said in a low voice, and swiveled her around so she faced me, "you didn't fuck four guys; *they* raped *you*. You've got to stop making this out like it's your fault."

She laughed once and it nearly broke me. "Whose fault is it, Beez? Those guys? Why would it be their fault? They were just acting on my suggestion. I told everyone I was going to get

133

with them, and apparently, I did. I'm surprised it was only four. Kind of a short train ride, all things considered."

Her words punctured through me and I almost got up to leave. How much more was I going to have to stomach? Four guys fucked *my* girlfriend. I almost envied Ani her ability to shut down all her emotions. Mine were clawing at me from the inside and tearing me apart.

"Of course it's their fault. They raped you. Don't you get it? I don't give a shit what you said at that party. You were either drunk or on some sort of roofie high and only a complete scumbag would ever screw around with you in that state."

Her eyes remained empty. Nothing I said was getting through to her. I gripped her shoulder too hard, wanting to shake some sense into her.

Kate finally said, "Ani, it's still considered rape if you weren't fully conscious. You didn't really make those decisions. You have to be sober to consent. Beth said that in the ER. Ben's right. This wasn't your fault."

A flash of pain crossed Ani's face and tears lined the edges of her eyelashes. Her chin trembled and I closed my eyes to it. I was wrong. Watching her fall apart was even worse than watching the emptiness. She probably needed to do it, but I didn't think I was ready for it. Not in the cafeteria. Not in front of all the assholes who'd been talking about her for the past few weeks.

She pulled her hand from mine and patted me. Moved her hand over my bald head like she'd done so many times before. "It's okay. It's going to be okay. I'm lucky I don't remember anything. It's easier that way."

Ani was trying to reassure me. I felt like an asshole. She wanted to make things better for *me*. This was exactly why she didn't want to tell her mom. I was completely worthless to her. I stood up from the table, kissed her on the cheek, and walked outside without another word.

16

I drove to Morton High School and sat in the parking lot trying to figure out what I was going to do. I couldn't just go up to a random guy and ask what he'd heard about the Manhole. Whoever told Ani in gym class could've been wrong. And I didn't think I could stomach talking about the things Ani had done or what had been done to her. But I needed to know the truth. It'd been eating away at me for too damn long.

When the final bell rang, people poured into the parking lot like thousands of carpenter ants. They sounded really loud to me, but it could have been because I'd been waiting in silence since I pulled into the lot. I watched a group of guys walking toward a beat-up white van. One of them started to hump the air like he had a girl pinned beneath him. In a quick move, I jumped out of my car and approached, my feet crunching over the remains of a broken iced tea bottle.

The other guys were laughing at his pantomime as I walked up. I narrowed my eyes and watched.

"I'm telling you," the guy said, slapping the air and moving his hips, "the girl was so wet, it was like standing under Niagara Falls."

My fists clenched at my sides and I bent my knees into an attack stance. I almost wished for the pain of a bloody fight. Someone to beat up or someone who'd beat me up so at least it was real pain, not the rotting ache inside my chest all the time. Christ. What was happening to me?

The guy finally noticed I'd joined the group. "What's up, bro?"

"Who are you talking about?" My body pulsed with rage. My teeth gnashed together. I was going to break a crown and piss off my mom again.

"My girlfriend. What's it to you?" he asked, taking a step back.

I relaxed slightly. What the hell was I doing? I was battling windmills.

"Nothing," I answered, and turned to my car. I took three steps, stopped for a second, and finally swiveled back to them. "Has anyone heard of the girl they're calling the Manhole?"

My knees nearly buckled from the weight of the word, but I locked them and searched each of the guys' faces. They exchanged looks and finally the guy who'd been describing his girlfriend shrugged.

"'Course. The chick who fucked a bunch of guys at a party and got off with a lighter afterward, right? What about her? You know her?"

I shut my eyes and nodded my head. "Were any of you guys there?"

More glances were exchanged. They were trying to figure out my motives, obviously. I didn't blame them. If any of them were one of the guys, I'd probably send him to the hospital.

"Not in the room with her," the humper said. "Those guys were from the city, I think. I was at the party, though."

"So you saw her?"

"Yeah, she was hanging all over the guys. She seemed pretty wasted. She flashed a bunch of them and then they took her upstairs." One of the guys standing close to me nodded.

"*They* took *her* upstairs?" I asked, trying to keep my voice steady.

"Well, yeah, I mean, she rode piggyback on some guy while another one held her ass from behind."

"Was she conscious?"

He nodded. "Yeah, she was into it, man. She was wasted but she was into it."

"Into it? You're sure? Not passed out?"

"No. Not passed out."

I didn't say anything so he continued.

"Could've been roofies, though. I've also seen chicks act like that when they're buzzing on Special K. There was a bunch of E going around the party too. You think this girl might've had some?"

I shook my head. "No. Not on purpose. Did you see them after?" My muscles were so tight, I didn't think I'd be able to swim for days.

"Yeah, a couple of guys came down talking about the show. They were the ones who called her the hot little Manhole. So are you gonna tell us why you care about this, bro? Who's this girl to you?"

I stared at each of them. They had formed a sort of semi-circle around me and my gaze kept darting between their pale faces, trying to figure out if any of them were responsible for what happened to Ani.

"She's my goddamn girlfriend," I spat out finally before stalking to my car. I didn't want to hear another "I'm sorry, man" and I didn't want them to ask me why I wasn't at the party. I kicked the half-broken bottle and ignored the mumbling from the guys behind me.

I slammed my car door and banged my head against the steering wheel. I couldn't shake the picture of Ani's arm linked around a stranger's neck while her ass filled the hands of someone else. I started the car, turned on the radio as loud as it could go, and peeled out of the parking lot.

Manhole. I was dating the Manhole.

I drove to Ani's house. I'd already be in a shitload of trouble with my mom for skipping the last three periods of school and an even bigger shitload of trouble with Coach for skipping practice again. I figured an extra hour wasn't going to make that big of a difference. Luckily, Gayle was teaching so I didn't have to pretend everything was fine.

"Where'd you go?" Ani asked when she ushered me into her room.

"Morton."

Ani froze. Her eyes enlarged and she wrapped her arms around her body. Little girl stance again. The one I'd hoped had gone away.

"Have you remembered anything more from the party, Ani?"

She shook her head and moved toward the bed. I sat down and pulled her next to me.

"Hasn't your mom asked about all these big clothes you've been wearing?" I fingered the sweatshirt that she'd worn almost every day for the past two weeks.

"No, I don't put on the sweatshirt until I get to school."

I wrapped my hand around her ponytail and she tugged away. My hand dropped and Ani must've felt bad because she nestled closer to me.

"What'd you hear at Morton?" she asked quietly.

"I think we should stop talking about this," I said, and tipped her face to mine. "We need to get on with our lives, and dwelling on whatever happened isn't going to make it better. You don't remember anything and I'm not going to trust a bunch of drunk guys at a party to fill me in on the details of the night."

"That bad, huh?"

"No." I took her hand and sandwiched it in both of mine. "Nothing we didn't suspect. They said it might've been roofies. I guess there was a lot of E going around the party too. But trying to figure all this out isn't going to help us move past it."

She looked at me and rubbed her free hand along the stubble of my head. "What do you think will help?"

I drew her closer and rested my hands along her hips, my fingers tracing her bones. "I think you were right. I think you need to be touched in a good way. I think you need to feel loved."

"Like have sex?"

"Yeah."

She blinked at me. I held my breath and she finally nodded.

I started to lift the sweatshirt over her head and stopped

when she trembled. "Do you not want to do this? Are you worried about your stitches?"

She shook her head and tried to pull the sweatshirt the rest of the way but the fabric kept slipping from her shaking hands.

"Maybe this isn't a good idea. If you're worried it will hurt, we can wait."

"It's fine. The doctor said the stitches dissolved and I'd healed fine," she said, at last removing the sweatshirt so she was just in a small T-shirt.

"If you . . ." I started.

She put her hand over my mouth. "Shh . . . I'm fine. The doctor said I'm fine. I just got the shivers for a second. It's kind of cold in here."

She pulled her shirt off and I rubbed her bare arms. I tugged my own shirt off and grabbed a condom from my wallet. She started to unbutton her jeans but I stopped her hands.

"We can go slow. We don't have to get right to it. I haven't really kissed you in weeks. Maybe we could start with that?" I asked.

She nodded and I put the condom on her table and lay on top of her, recalling the feeling of her from all the times before. The smell of her swirled around me, sugary mints and a little tangyness from her grapefruit lotion. My Ani.

"You've lost too much weight," I whispered, touching her rib cage.

"Food doesn't taste good anymore."

"You need to eat for me. I don't want you to waste away." I kissed her neck.

She turned her head and touched my chin. "Okay. I'll eat. For you."

I kissed her gently. My body couldn't help reacting when she rose up to meet me and stuck her tongue deep in my mouth. But she didn't flinch when she felt my hardness on her thigh, she just opened up and wrapped her legs around me. I could have cried in relief. I went as slow as I could, trying to forget the guys at Morton. Forget the lighter. Forget everything but the feel of Ani's skin. And when I finally slid inside her, I kissed her tears and whispered, "I love you" over and over again.

My mom stood at the front door when I got home.

"I thought you had class," I said, dropping my backpack onto the ground and heading for the kitchen.

"I did, but I got a call from your coach on the way out. He's worried about your chances of getting a scholarship," she said, following me.

I pulled open the fridge and took a long gulp from the orange juice bottle. She pursed her lips and pointed to the bottle.

I tucked it back in the fridge and turned to her, crossing my arms.

"And?"

"And why didn't you go to practice? Where were you?"

"With Ani," I said, and didn't break contact with her eyes.

"Do you think you might be spending too much time with this girl?"

I looked at her blankly. She let out a mom sigh.

"Don't get me wrong," she continued, "I like her, but you've never missed practice over a girl before."

"There's never been an Ani before."

She gave me another big mom sigh. "There's a lot going on right now, Ben. Your father has that new business pitch at work and I'm busting my butt at grad school while still trying to work and be a room parent in your brother's classroom. Please tell me I don't need to be worried about this relationship."

"You don't need to be worried about this relationship," I answered, and pushed away from the fridge, grabbing an apple from a basket on the counter.

"I don't want to have to approach your dad with this," she said.

I raised my shoulders. Dad protected his family above all else, but he was also fiercely loyal. If everything came out, he'd side with me. I had no doubt. Problem was, I didn't want everything to come out. Not like this, not with them.

Mom rifled through her purse, grumbling before finally pulling out a wad of money and handing it to me. "Can I trust you to take your brother to and from soccer practice tonight?"

"Of course," I said, pocketing the money. "I'm not a total screwup. But just so you know, Michael hates soccer. He's only doing it because you're making him."

"Soccer is good for him. He needs to get some fresh air and exercise instead of playing those video games all the time. Too much of something isn't good for anyone," she said, catching my eye.

I took a bite of apple and walked out of the room.

"That's twenty dollars for the two of you to grab dinner after practice. I expect change. I'm meeting your father after my class. We'll be home by ten. Make sure you do your homework," she called after me.

"Whatever you say," I mumbled, and picked up my backpack before heading to my room.

"How was soccer?"

Michael hopped in the Jeep looking way too clean and sweat free.

"Stupid. I might as well be the water boy. They had me play backup goalie."

I shook my head. "Dude, you have to show some effort or they're gonna keep having you do that kind of shit."

"I don't care. Maybe Mom won't sign me up for it anymore, then."

I started to say something but shut my mouth. What the hell did I care?

"We going for pizza?" Michael asked. He'd pulled out his DS and was already playing some Mario game.

"Yep."

"Mom told me Tati Marie got a job."

"Really?" I asked, throwing my car into first. I'd almost forgotten the conversation when my dad mentioned she was having a hard time. It seemed so long ago.

"Yeah. Dad found it for her. She's working in a dentist's office."

"Huh." One less thing for my parents to stress about, at least.

We drove the rest of the two miles in silence with the exception of the beeps and bings from Michael's game. I pulled into the lot and flipped Michael's DS shut.

"Can we eat here?" he asked.

I was about to nod when I saw Gayle standing at the counter of the pizza place. Guilt sucker punched me. Shit. Would I look like a complete idiot if I put the car in reverse and drove away?

Michael bounded out of the car and pulled my door open. He followed my eyes.

"Who's that?"

I shrugged and pushed him toward the pizza place

entrance. It reeked of grease and pepperoni and my stomach grumbled. Bubblegum pop music was being piped through the speakers and the girl at the register was frantically texting. We walked up to the counter as Gayle fumbled with her wallet. She was wearing one of Ani's shirts.

"Ben," she said. "What are you doing here? And who's this?" She smiled in that preschool teacher way and Michael grinned back at her. At least he understood sucking up.

"This is my brother, Michael. We were just grabbing a pizza for dinner. Our parents are out tonight. Where's Ani?"

"Well," she said, and laughed, "she was in the midst of the world's longest shower when I got home so I decided to grab us dinner on my own. That girl and her showers. I swear it's gotten worse since she met you." She looked at me pointedly and I blushed.

"I'm not sure why she's so worried about smelling nice all the time," she continued. "You'd think she'd take better care of her room and her clothes if it was that big of a deal."

Doubt pushed its way into my brain, but I shook it off. Ani *had* always been into long showers.

"Well, I better go before our dinner gets cold. It was nice seeing you, Ben. And nice to meet you, Michael." She gave him a little wink and smiled at me. I smiled back and ignored the truth gnawing at me, the desire to put all this on someone else.

We drove home with the music too loud to talk. Michael's

choice, so some classical station. It didn't matter. It didn't drown out the questions in my head. Or the memory of Ani's tears when we had sex.

I wolfed down the pizza and went to my room. Ani's painting hung slightly tilted on the wall, a reminder and accusation all at once. Ani never painted anymore. She hadn't stayed after in the school art room since the party. I wanted to ask her about it, but I was afraid to. Afraid of her answer. Afraid that I'd have to add yet another thing to the list of what the rape had taken from her.

I called her, but she didn't pick up. The minute her voice mail beeped, I babbled into the phone, "That was nice today. Maybe. Was it? Was it okay? I love you. I'm sorry. I hope it was okay. I hope you're okay. It was nice. I hope things are better now. I love you. Fuck. Sorry. I'll see you tomorrow."

17

Ani came to school the next day without the big sweatshirt on. I almost whooped like an asshole when I saw her in a white short-sleeved T-shirt and jeans. She marched up to me and gave me a full-on kiss. Full-on. Nice.

"Whoa," I said with a dopey grin. "What was that for?"

She smiled and slid herself underneath my arm. "No reason. Just thanking you, I guess. I got your message. It's okay. It's good."

I pulled back and looked at her. She was sort of buzzing, like she'd had too many cups of coffee or hadn't slept. Her eyes darted past me to the end of the hall, where a bunch of guys were gathered watching us.

"You don't have to thank me."

Her hand grazed the back of my head and she tugged on my ear.

"That tickles." My shoulders lifted and I batted her hand away from my ear.

"Sorry. I've missed touching your sexy baldness."

I smiled. My Ani had been returned to me. Thank Christ for that. If I wasn't worried she'd get the wrong message, I might have dropped to my knees and said a prayer of gratitude.

Her eyes shifted back to the guys and I followed the movement.

"Do you know them?" I asked.

"Not really," she said, and kissed me again. She lifted her leg and wrapped it around the back of my thighs, drawing me closer and grinding into me. I didn't pull back because it felt so good to kiss her again, but we weren't really a hallway PDA couple so it was kind of weird.

"How come they keep looking at you?" I asked after breaking the kiss.

She shrugged and pulled me in the other direction. I looked back one more time, but the guys had fist-bumped and dispersed.

"Meet me at lunch?" Ani asked, hooking her finger into the waist of my jeans.

"Of course." I turned toward class and she headed up the stairs. I watched her climb the steps and ignored the weird feeling that curled in my stomach. Why had she worn the super-tight jeans?

. . .

Ani had her hand on my lap for most of lunch. I couldn't really figure out what was behind her need to constantly touch me, but I wasn't going to call her on it after she finally seemed to be moving past the rape.

Kevin came over and smiled approvingly at Ani's appearance. I raised an eyebrow at him but he lifted a shoulder. I couldn't really blame him, she'd been wearing the big sweatshirt for too long.

"When are you all out on parole?" he asked, sliding into the seat across from us and looking from me to Ani.

"My mom caved and gave me my walking papers, but Beez may be in for life," Ani answered. I dropped my hand to hers and she curled her fingers around mine. Soft fingers, shaking, but maybe with the same excitement I was feeling.

"Yeah, even on good behavior, I'm grounded for at least two more weeks."

Kevin shook his head. "Sucks to be you, dude. Massive party at Watson's house this weekend."

I tensed and glanced at Ani. Her eyes had gotten a bit buzzier, but she didn't react otherwise. Just squeezed my hand tighter.

"Looks like you'll have to go solo on that one," I said to Kevin.

"I'll go," Kate chimed in from the end of the table. She had been frantically studying for a trig test and I didn't realize she was even listening. Her hair curtained over her face and she bit the skin on the edge of her thumb.

"Me too," Ani said.

Kevin's head whipped up and I opened my mouth to say something, but Ani put her free hand over my lips.

"I'm not going to hide away for the rest of high school because of some crazy shit that happened at a party. You said yourself that I needed to start moving past this."

"Not by going to another party," I argued.

"I'll be fine. I won't drink and I'll stay by Kevin the whole night."

I looked at Kevin. He let out a loud breath and raised his shoulders.

"I won't let anything happen to her. You know I'll keep my eye on her."

I snorted. "Yeah, I'll bet." I switched my focus to Ani. "I don't think this is a good idea. Are you sure you want to go? You don't have to prove anything to us."

She released my hand and let hers slide up my thigh. Whoa, was she going to grope me in front of everyone? I grabbed her hand and stilled it.

She leaned into me and whispered, "Yes, I want to do this."

I shifted in my suddenly uncomfortable jeans. "I'm going with you."

152

She shook her head. "You're grounded. Your mom won't let you out."

"I'll figure out a way to sneak out. When do you want to meet?"

Kevin shrugged but didn't offer any more opinions. "Party starts at nine. We'll probably head around ten. Want me to pick the girls up?"

I nodded. "Yeah and don't let either of them drink. And don't go getting wasted yourself. They are your responsibility until I get there."

I thought the girls might argue, but neither Kate nor Ani said anything. Ani started to pick at her lunch and Kate returned to her trig cramming. I gave Kevin one last look and choked down the rest of my sandwich.

18

On the drive home from school, I asked Ani if she wanted to come over. I was already late for swim practice, and I didn't care if I skipped it again if it meant spending time with her. She told me she had too much stuff to do. If she hadn't hopped in my lap and tried to dry hump me in front of her place, I might have thought she was blowing me off. As it was, I had to pull around the corner so we weren't completely on display.

"What's going on with all the touching?" I asked, trying to pry her hands away from the button of my jeans while she nibbled on my neck.

"It's like you said, I need to be loved. It's comforting having your hands on me."

I traced my fingers along her jaw and tilted her face toward mine. Her eyes still looked weird.

"You're sort of going from zero to sixty here. I'm not really a PDA kind of guy, and I didn't think you were a PDA kind of girl either. I mean, we weren't . . . before."

She stilled for a second and then started to pull herself off my lap. I held her hips so she couldn't leave. Her eyes squeezed shut and she took a slow breath.

"Maybe I'm more of a PDA girl than you think. I did make out with a guy at a party full of people. And if rumors are correct, I screwed a lighter in front of a bunch of guys as well."

"You were wasted," I retorted, gripping her hips tighter. "And you didn't screw a lighter. Those pricks left a lighter inside of you. Why are you turning this on yourself?"

She shook her head back and forth. "I'm not getting into this again with you. We said we were going to move past it."

She dug her nails into my hands so I had to release her.

"What do you want from me?" I asked. I tried to hide the anguish in my voice, but she must have heard it. Her hand rubbed my cheek.

"Nothing, Beez. I don't want anything from you."

"Ani . . ." I started, but she turned away and opened the door to get out. A cold wind rushed across my face.

"I'll call you later," she said, and waved me off. "Have a good practice."

I knew she wouldn't call, and it took everything I had not to go after her and shake her.

I went back to school and got reamed by Coach for being late again. He made me swim an extra hour and told me I better pull my shit together because my times were worse than ever. He threatened to kick me off the team and I almost didn't care.

A message from Beth, the rape counselor, was on my phone when I got out of practice. I ignored it and drove home too fast, listening to music too loud. Hard, fast guitar, pounding drums, and lots of screeching.

In my room, I stared at my homework for an hour without doing one thing. My body hurt, but I couldn't rest because different thoughts kept zinging through my head.

I choked down a warmed-up bowl of soup and listened to Michael's latest clarinet piece, but nothing stopped my toxic thoughts. I finally called Beth back on the cell number she'd left.

"Ben?" she asked. She sounded tired.

"Sorry. I should have called back during your work hours."

"It's okay," she answered. "I was just calling because I wanted to check in. It's sort of protocol for us. And I couldn't get through to Ani."

"Oh. Okay. I'm good, thanks."

"So, is everything okay with Ani?"

"I don't know. She's better, I think. I don't know. She's a little weird right now."

"A little weird is probably normal for rape survivors," Beth said, and I heard her switch into counselor mode. "Rape trauma syndrome can look really different for different people."

"Oh. Okay." Why had I bothered calling her back? Everything she said was textbook bullshit.

"So did you want to talk about it? Or anything else you might have questions about?"

"Well, I don't know. I guess things are just a little weird, that's all." I should have hung up. I knew it. But it was like the phone was glued to the side of my head and her voice on the other end seemed so full of answers.

"What's weird? What are you seeing?"

Did I want to get into this with her? Crap. I didn't really have anyone else. God, Ani had boxed me. Boxed us both in.

"Well," I said, sitting back against my pillows. "She seems to have gotten over the whole shutting-down thing, but now . . . I don't know. It's hard to explain. She seems kind of off."

"How so?"

"She's really touchy," I blurted out. What the hell kind of complaint was that? I sounded like a frickin' baby.

"Touchy like prickly?" Beth asked.

"No," I mumbled, "more like she can't keep her hands off me."

"Oh. Well, that can happen," Beth said, and somehow her tone of voice made me feel like it actually was normal. It wasn't her usual rape counselor tone, more like a friend. Or maybe I just wanted that from her so now I couldn't tell the difference. "Some survivors become clingy to the people they love. It's like they're grieving over almost losing them, especially with violent sexual assault. In Ani's case, she might be clinging to you because you represent a normal life for her."

"I'm not so sure this is us being normal," I said.

"If she still has so many holes in her memory, you are constant and solid for her and she needs that right now. Clingy is really normal."

"Well, yeah, I guess you'd call it clingy. But it's sort of more than that," I started. How was I going to explain my fears to Beth?

"More?"

"Yeah, like she wants me to be with her . . . intimately . . . if you get what I mean." I was like a fricking *Dr. Phil* head case. Crybaby chump. My thumb moved to the off button, but I waited to press it, wincing in anticipation of her rape counselor tone clicking back into place.

"Oh," she said.

"'Oh'? That's all you got? 'Oh'? Are they paying you the big bucks for these responses?" I joked. It was the only way to brush off the fact that I was a total dumb ass complaining about my girlfriend being unable to keep her hands off me.

Beth chuckled a little. "Sorry, I didn't think that's where

you were going with this conversation. But it is pretty common, too. For Ani, maybe being intimate with you is empowering to her."

"Will you stop with the counselor speak already? And stop telling me everything is normal or common? What does that even mean?"

Beth sighed. "Maybe Ani feels safe because she's the one in control, deciding who to be with and how far she wants to go. You are a safe person for her to be with. You're not going to hurt her."

"Huh. I hadn't thought of it like that. I guess that makes sense. But what am I supposed to do about it?"

"Does being with her like that make you uncomfortable because of the assault?" she asked in a soft voice.

"No, of course not. I just . . . I mean, it's really different for me. Ani and I had been together before, but I'm not really used to her being all over me. Not in front of everyone. I'm not against it, but I feel like it's weird for her. She wasn't like that before. Or at least not so much."

"Okay, well, here's my counselor take on it: I'd recommend trying to talk to her about it in a way that isn't judgmental, but more just points out that it's different for you guys. You also need to make clear that you respect her choices and want to empower her in any way that you can. You don't have to call it empowering her, but let her know that she's the boss of her own body. If you're not comfortable with the intimacy, establish some boundaries with her, but make sure she doesn't feel like you're rejecting her because of the rape."

"Um, okay," I said. How the hell was I supposed to do all that?

"And please encourage her to join one of our support groups or, at the very least, contact someone on the hotline number I gave her."

"Okay, I'll try. Thanks."

"Ben?"

"Yeah?"

"You can call me again too. You've got my cell number."

"Okay."

I hung up and looked at my ceiling. Ani wasn't going to call a hotline or join a support group. She'd barely talked to me about what happened and she was dating me. She wasn't about to talk to a roomful of strangers about something she couldn't remember. I sighed and tried to call her. No answer. My head started to ache. Why did everything have to be so hard?

19

I was late for Watson's party, of course. I had to wait forever for my parents to go to bed so I could sneak out. They decided to stay up to watch the local news. I sat on the edge of my bed, tapping my toes and texting Kevin to remind him to keep an eye on Ani. After my third text, he messaged back: *Chill the fuck out. I've got her. She's fine.*

It was past eleven o'clock by the time I got there. I walked in and scanned the crowd. It was packed mostly with people I knew, which was good. There was a sweaty mass of too-close couples moving on the dance floor. It was a bakery with all the bodies inside. Dim lights and loud music. But still I found Ani within three minutes of entering. She had on a short skirt and strappy top. My heart stuttered. She stood by the keg with a cup in her hand, talking to a group of people. Kevin had his arm wrapped tightly around her.

I made a beeline toward them and pulled her to the side.

"Ben," she said, and jumped into my arms. The contents of her cup sloshed down my back.

"I thought you weren't going to drink," I said, and tried to set her down. She clung tighter.

"It's water," she said, and drank what was left in the cup before tossing it aside. She moved her mouth onto mine and I tasted the cool cleanness of the water.

Kevin sauntered over to us.

"See? Perfectly safe. I told you I'd look out for her, dude."

I wanted to wipe the smug smile off his face, but I didn't want to say anything in front of Ani. She hadn't taken my beating up the asshole in the hall at school very well and I didn't think she'd appreciate me going off on Kevin and the previous placement of his hand on her hip.

She unwrapped one of her arms from my neck and hooked it around Kevin so she was sandwiched between us. I tried to pull her away but she held tight.

"He totally kept his eyes on me the whole time. He was like a stand-in boyfriend."

"Nice," I grumbled, and gave him my ass-kicking stare.

"He's been very accommodating, watching out for me when he could have been trolling for girls. I think I should reward him," she continued without even noticing my reaction.

I tugged at her some more, but she released me and wrapped both her arms around Kevin. I saw his eyes bug out for half a second before her mouth was on his and her leg snaked up and pulled him toward her.

What. The. Fuck.

"Ani!" I shouted, and grabbed her shoulder so hard she stumbled away from Kevin.

She turned on me and crossed her arms, pillowing up her boobs so I could almost see the nipples popping out of her tiny shirt.

"What?" she snapped.

I took a breath and looked at Kevin. His hand covered his mouth and he stared at me in panic. He shook his head at my accusatory face and I zeroed in on Ani.

"Can I talk to you outside?" I asked in a low voice. I didn't want a big showdown in front of everyone. Ani already had a reputation at parties and I didn't want to make things worse for her. But my brain was reeling.

I seethed and pointed to the deck door. She raised her chin and stomped out in front of me. When I had closed the door behind me, I turned my anger on her.

"Is this your way of breaking up with me?" I spat.

Her eyes got buzzy again and she shook her head. "I'm not breaking up with you. Why would you think that?"

"I don't know, maybe because you started making out with my best friend in front of me."

"I was saying thank you for keeping me safe," she snapped back.

"By kissing him?"

"Yes, Beezus, in case you haven't heard from the *entire* school, that's what I do."

I scrubbed my hand over my face and massaged my temples. She moved her hands over her shoulders, trying to keep warm in the cold night air. I looked at her outfit again and cringed at the amount of skin she had on display.

"Why are you being this way? You're killing me here. I want to help you, but you're making it so hard for me."

"I didn't ask for your help."

"Ani," I said, and rubbed my hands across her shoulders.

"I didn't even want you at the hospital." Her words stung me like tiny razors across my skin.

I bit the inside of my cheek and remembered the things Beth had said.

"It's your choice. All of this. It's *your* choice. Do you still want to be with me?"

"I never said I didn't," she said, taking a small step closer.

"Then be with *me*. Don't screw around with Kevin. I don't want to share you. I'm not that guy. You know I'm not."

She stood on her toes and kissed the top of my head. She

moved down my cheek to my neck and sucked on it like she wanted to give me a hickey. Her arms hooked around me and she lifted herself up so I had to hold her beneath her thighs. I could feel the goose bumps on the backs of her legs.

"Poor, poor Beezus. Don't you realize? You already have shared me."

She kissed me on the mouth then, deep and long. I wanted to break away, talk to her more, try to work out what had happened, but she clung to me so desperately, I couldn't stop. I moved her off the deck and into the darkness on the side of the house. She pulled frantically at my clothes and I quickly unzipped my jeans and rolled a condom on while she slipped her panties off. What the hell was I doing?

I almost retreated but her voice pleaded and I didn't know what to do. Was this what Beth meant by empowering Ani? Because all I could see was a whole lot of screwed-up.

20

I got home from practice the next Monday afternoon and my brother was in front of the TV playing Xbox.

"Hey, shrimp," I said, dropping down next to him. "How was rehearsal?"

"Okay," he mumbled, maneuvering his hand over the controls without looking at me.

"Mom at class?"

He nodded again. The loud explosions from the game made me flinch.

"Michael," I said, "put down the frickin' controller. Mom's told you a hundred times, it's rude to keep playing when people are talking to you."

He paused the game and stared at the screen.

"What's up? What's wrong with you?"

He slowly turned his head. "What's wrong with *you*?"

"Nothing," I said.

He barked a laugh and picked up his controller again. I grabbed it from him and sat on it.

"What the heck? Give it back."

"What's your problem?" I asked.

His face flashed hurt. "You used to talk to us. Now you're always in your room. Or with Ani."

It was Michael's attempt at a verbal slap, and somehow it cut so much deeper than any of the lectures Mom poured out.

"What are you talking about?"

"Don't act like I'm dumb. You used to talk to us and you don't anymore. Not about anything real. I don't know what happened or what's wrong, but you don't talk to us anymore."

A coil of guilt wove its way into my stomach. Michael was worried about me. Mom and Dad were worried about me. I felt like a piece of crap. And still, I couldn't say anything. Not to my parents. Definitely not to Michael. This wasn't their problem.

"I have no idea what you mean. Everything is fine."

Michael shrugged. Had he picked up that indifference from me? "If that's how you wanna be, go ahead and lie. I thought we were brothers. I thought we could tell each other anything."

I searched Michael's face. His chin trembled. It made me

want to cry seeing how hard he was trying to keep it together.

"Sometimes it's better to do things on your own. I still love you guys. But this is my shit, not yours, to deal with," I said finally.

A small smile crossed his face. "I get that. Sort of. It's like how I didn't want to tell Mom I'm not really playing soccer, just sitting on the sides. But you could tell *me* if you wanted to."

I opened my mouth to say something, but then decided against it. I was a disappointment as a brother and I didn't have any right to screw up his happiness with my own shitstorm. I mentally kicked myself. If Michael guessed something was wrong, I was doing a crap job of holding things together.

I considered again talking to my dad. Coming clean about things. But as the echo of Ani's pleas against telling her mom circled through my mind, I realized I couldn't say anything to him about what happened at the party. About what was happening with us now. Because as soon as my dad found out, any chance of Ani and me ever being normal again would be tossed out the window.

"Sorry I can't get into it with you, shrimp," I said at last. I gave him his Xbox controller and picked up the other one, then settled deeper into the couch next to him, waiting for him to respond. He didn't say anything.

The Sunday after Thanksgiving, I was finally ungrounded. It was a seventy-five-degree day and my mom announced over breakfast she couldn't stand seeing me inside moping any longer. I bolted to my room and texted Ani.

We went for ice cream to celebrate and I was determined not to make our date end in sex. It's not that I minded, but it seemed it was the only way Ani and I had connected since the party and I missed just hanging out with her. Every time we started talking about anything remotely real, she withdrew or jumped me. I was starting to get kind of messed up about it.

I held her hand as we walked through town and told her stories about times my friends and I had done stupid shit when we were young. She smiled and patted my arm but looked in front of her without any other response.

"Hey, what's a cow's favorite movie?" I asked when we sat on a bench in front of Peterson's Ice Cream.

She looked at me with a real smile and light in her eyes. My breath stopped. God, she was beautiful.

"*The Sound of Moosic*," I finished.

"Oh my God, you're such a dork. I heard that joke in the third grade."

"Okay, how about this one?" I asked, hanging on to the familiarity between us. "What do you call a cow on a pogo stick?"

She snorted and my heart sped up.

"A milk shake!" she said, and laughed. "Seriously, Beez, you need to stop getting your material from the elementary school playground."

I nudged her shoulder and tugged on one of her braids. If I hadn't been watching closely, I might've missed when she closed up again. But I saw it in her face and I hated her for not being able to hold on to our laughter. And I hated myself for being angry about it.

"Is something bothering you?" I finally asked after too much silence.

"No."

"You got quiet all of a sudden," I said hesitantly.

"You have some strawberry on the corner of your mouth," she said, and before I could wipe it away, her tongue darted out of her mouth to lick it. She tried to linger on my lips, but I pulled away.

"Is something bothering *you*?" she asked, pouting.

"No. I just wanted to talk to you."

"Why?" She leaned away from me and gave me a suspicious look. I pulled her back into my side.

"'Cause things have been kind of different with us. We used to talk more. I'm not trying to be judgmental or whatever, but I've noticed."

"Beezus, don't you know I can put my mouth to way better use than talking?" She batted her eyelashes, which might have been cute if they weren't framing dead eyes.

I got up and tossed my ice cream in the garbage can. My hands clenched at my sides.

"Why do you say shit like that? Huh? Do you say that kind of thing to other people?"

"Are you jealous?" she asked. I wanted to smack the mean out of her. It wasn't her fault, but I didn't care. She couldn't hold on to old Ani and it pissed me off.

"Not jealous. Tired of it. You're more than this. Better than this. Don't you get it?"

Tears filled her eyes, but she blinked them away. She tossed her ice cream toward the garbage can, but it fell short and landed in a lump of pistachio on the sidewalk.

"You know what? We're done. I can't do this with you anymore. It's too exhausting," she said, turning away from me.

"What? What's so goddamn exhausting?" I yelled, and kicked the garbage can.

"You are. We are. I can't be with you. It takes too much out of me."

A hole the size of a missile formed in my stomach.

"You're breaking up with me?"

"Yes," she answered, and dropped her head.

I took a step toward her. I pulled on a piece of hair that had fallen from her braid.

"No. You're not." I lifted her chin.

"You can't say no. If someone wants to break up, you have to let them." Her voice shook.

"I *can* say no. I'm saying it. No. You're not leaving me. I'm not leaving you." I hadn't gone through all this shit to have her walk away from me.

"You're tired of me. You said you were," she protested, but her eyes didn't have any fight in them.

"I didn't say that. I said I was tired of you putting yourself down, acting like all you are is some sex object."

She curled into me and buried her face in my chest. I felt the wetness of tears through my T-shirt. I hushed her and stroked her hair. Nothing I did stopped her crying. After several minutes, I heard her take a deep breath. She pulled back and faced me.

"Okay, if you won't let me break up with you, you have to stop judging me."

"I'm not judging you, Ani," I argued.

"Yes, you are. Everyone's judging me. It's like they're all waiting to see what I'll do next. They're waiting for me to fall."

"No, they're not."

"You have no idea what it's like. I walk into a room and people stop talking. I walk down the hall and all I hear are whispers of 'Firecrotch' and 'Manhole.' And the worst part is, I can't say shit to defend myself. I've got nothing but a giant fricking void about that night and a bunch of people telling me what I said and did."

"It was one night. You can't let it define you."

Silence sat between us.

"What am I going to do, Ben?" she finally asked.

I almost broke in two hearing her sound so defeated. I wished I could make it all go away. I'd never wanted anything so much. But it took all this energy to hold the pieces of her together. It would cost us both something. It already had.

Her face started to crumple and I gripped her tighter. "I'll make this better, baby. I'll make you better. I promise."

She gave me a sad smile and the air between us shifted. I had no idea how to keep the promise. We both knew it. The fault lay on me and the reality of her actually "getting better" inched further away. If only I could really fix things.

We went back to my car and had sex because I didn't know what else to do when she slipped her pants off and straddled me. It was like I was outside of myself. Watching. Seeing how things really were with us. But I couldn't stop it from happening. We didn't even kiss when we were doing it. Ani fake moaned and panted. And I let her. Her eyes stared past me to the back window. Glazed and vacant. I came and pulled the condom off quickly. My stomach heaved and I swallowed the bile in my throat. My hands shook in self-disgust. I was exactly like all those guys. I had just fucked the Manhole.

21

I wouldn't be with Ani alone for the next three weeks. I couldn't. I made up excuses about why I couldn't come over and pretended not to see the hurt expression on her face. I swam before and after school and still couldn't get back to my record times. Coach looked at his stopwatch and mumbled to himself, but thankfully didn't say anything.

I went to lunch with Ani, Kate, and Kevin. I made sure I always sat across from Ani. Sometimes other people sat with us. We acted like nothing was wrong, but Kevin met my eyes in question several times. I shook my head and didn't say anything about what was happening with her. What was happening with us.

One lunch, Ani didn't show up. I went looking for her but couldn't find her. When I finally did, she was coming out of the handicap bathroom on the second floor. She got a weird look when she saw me and started tugging on her shirt. When I asked her where she'd been, she turned away and didn't say anything.

I took her hand and walked back to the cafeteria with her. A guy followed us in and brushed too long against Ani as he passed. I started to say something to him, but Ani stopped me with an openmouthed kiss and her hands on my ass. I pulled away and ducked my head so I wouldn't have to see the stares of the entire cafeteria. Ani dropped her hands and moved slowly toward the lunch line.

I tumbled into bed every night sore from practice, from swimming wrong, sitting wrong, moving wrong. My body didn't seem to fit me anymore. I wasn't aware of how I moved in the way I used to be. Instead, my mind pushed me from place to place.

Ani's recovery meant everything and nothing all at the same time. I couldn't stop thinking about her, seeing the vacancy on her face as she stared out the car window, but I couldn't cross the bridge between us. I was just a guy. Nothing I did or said made any difference. And for as much as I wanted to be there for her, I couldn't ignore the resentment taking up residence in my stomach.

The Friday before winter break, I saw Ani in the hall surrounded by guys. The haze that had been clouding me for weeks vanished into red-hot fury. I stalked toward them, afraid they were saying shit to her, but she stood smiling and laughing.

"What's up?" I asked as I approached.

"Hey, Beez," she said in a phony high voice. She batted her glassy eyes at me. Fake interest like how Morgan used to look at me. "We were all just making plans for winter break."

"All of you?" I scanned the faces of the guys. Big guys. Bigger than me. Most of them stared at me smugly. What the hell had Ani done?

"Well, you've been so busy . . ." Ani looked at me pointedly. Shit. These were my choices? Pretend everything was okay between us or let her hang out with a bunch of guys over break doing God knows what?

"You have plans with me over winter break. These guys will have to find their fun somewhere else," I said, clenching my hands.

She slithered toward me and wrapped her arms around my neck. I tried not to flinch as the guys smirked at her ridiculous display.

I grabbed her wrist and pulled her away from the guys.

"This is it? This is what we are? This is what you are?" I asked once we had moved away from our audience.

She blinked her eyes. They didn't seem to be focusing very well. Was she high? That too? Although maybe it would be better if she was, then I wouldn't have to feel like I brought about the deadness.

"You're not supposed to judge me," she said.

"And you're not supposed to act like a whore," I retorted. She reeled back and I banged my fist into the locker beside me. God, everything sucked.

I inhaled. "I'm sorry. I didn't mean that." I pulled her closer but her body didn't react. Her clothes were obnoxiously skimpy for winter.

"You wouldn't let me break up with you," she said in a flat voice.

"And I still won't. But this shit is ridiculous. What do you hope to accomplish with all this?"

"I make the choice about what I want to do with my body," she said, and her chin tilted up slightly. It was actually a relief to see defiance in her eyes after so much void.

"That's right. You do. But is this really what you want? Is this what I deserve?" I held her face and looked into her eyes, searching. Her pupils darted around, refusing to engage with me. I tapped her cheek to get her to focus.

"What does it matter what I want or what you deserve? This is who I am," she said, and pulled away from me. She turned her back and said, "I'll be around. My mom is teaching a winter-break art camp. Come over if you want. Or don't." Her head finally swiveled and her emotionless face met mine. "I'm at your disposal."

• • •

Kevin showed up at my house after swim practice. I'd been expecting him to have a talk with me ever since Ani jumped him at Watson's party, but he had waited. I couldn't tell if it was because he felt bad or because he didn't want to add to my stress over her.

"You're in a shit spiral with Ani, dude," he said as soon as I opened my door.

"No kidding."

"I didn't want to be the one to tell you this, but I didn't think you'd want to be a chump any longer. She's screwing around with other guys. Not just flirting. Screwing around with them for real."

I closed my eyes and took some deep breaths like I tried to do before swim races. They didn't work. I wanted to rip someone's head off. I turned on Kevin, but the look of pity in his face made me punch the door instead. My mom called from the kitchen to see what the racket was about. I told her it was fine and pushed Kevin outside to the garage. Boxes were stacked neatly against one of the walls, and the bikes Michael and I never rode were anchored on hooks from the ceiling.

"She wants to break up with me," I told him. I brushed away a cobweb that stuck to my arm when I leaned against the wall.

"Then let her, dude. She's making you look bad."

"I can't leave her after everything that's happened. I don't play that way," I said.

"Did you even hear me? She's screwing around with other guys. You got to get out of this." He looked like he wanted to smack me upside the head.

"I heard what you said, but you don't understand. I fricking let her go to that party on her own. She never would've done any of that shit if I were there. This is on me. It's my job to take care of her."

"Yeah, I'd get that if you were married to her, maybe. But she's your girlfriend. You're eighteen. You aren't responsible for her," he retorted.

"She's still Ani," I said.

"She's a messed-up version of Ani. That's not the girl who told you your hair made you look like an asshole. It's time to cut her loose."

I kicked a box and turned on him. "No. I'm not walking away from her. That's a total dick move. She's screwed up because a bunch of guys messed with her and left a lighter inside of her. She doesn't deserve for me to bail on her."

Kevin raised his hands. "Okay, peace. Don't shoot the messenger. I understand, but listen, I'm not the only one saying you should get out of this. I mean, I get that messed-up shit happened at that party, but what the hell? How many guys are you going to let on that train?"

I fisted my hands. "How many guys are on it right now?"

I'd had my head up my ass. I suspected shit was going down

with other guys, but I didn't want to believe it. I didn't want to fucking share her and I hated that the guys who raped her got her too. But my anger just made everything she'd accused me of even more true. I couldn't stand what we were becoming, but I couldn't be the guy to walk away. For me or for Ani.

Kevin shook his head. "I don't know. I heard some of the lacrosse guys saying something about her in a janitor's closet. I didn't hear too much, but they referred to her as the hot lacrosse train whore."

Heat poured through me. Firecrotch. Manhole. Cum Dumpster. Train whore. The words pounded in my head like a sledgehammer.

"Son of a bitch. What am I supposed to do?"

"I think you should talk to her mom," Kevin said.

I'd considered it. Every day. More than once. Gayle was like a friend and I knew she'd probably be more help to Ani than I'd been. But every time I thought of doing it, I imagined the betrayal Ani would feel. She'd told me over and over how she didn't want her mom involved. How her mom would only make things worse. And it didn't really feel like my secret to tell.

"I can't do that, dude. I'll lose Ani for good."

Kevin shook his head. "You've lost her already. This shit is bigger than you. You gotta talk to someone. You're not gonna fix her or make her better. And honestly, dude, who do you think you are to even try?"

"Her goddamn boyfriend," I said, seething.

"Which makes you what? Her fricking shrink? She's out of control. She's not going to let you rein that shit in. It's not how she works."

I took a step back and pressed my head against the garage wall. "I know. You're right. That counselor Beth told me she was re-empowering herself or whatever by making her own choices about her body. I keep trying to remember that. I don't want to take that away from her even though it means she's crapping on everything we have."

"Well," Kevin said, and put his hand on my shoulder, "you should probably call Beth again. Because this isn't empowering; this is bullshit. The only thing she's doing is living up to her reputation as the Manhole."

22

I couldn't find Beth's cell phone number, so I called the number for her organization that I found on the website.

"Oh," the woman on the phone said, "Beth's one of our ER volunteers. She doesn't work here. Is there someone else I can put you on the phone with? Or can I transfer you to our crisis hotline?"

"She doesn't work for you?" What the hell?

"Well, she does, but as a volunteer. Most of our ER advocates are volunteers. If you'd like, I can let her know you called."

"Yeah. Okay. Yeah." Beth wasn't even a real crisis counselor. She was a *volunteer*. God. No wonder she sounded like she was reading off a script. She wasn't even really qualified to help me. My stomach bottomed out.

. . .

"You're a volunteer?" I said as soon as Beth called me that night. "Why did you act like you work for that rape organization?"

"Because I do. I take hospital ER shifts once or twice a month." No apology. Just matter-of-fact.

"That's bullshit. You acted like you had some experience. Like you knew what you were doing. Like you could actually help me."

"I can help you. I've been trained as a volunteer. It was a really extensive training. They don't just slot us in ERs and tell us good luck."

It felt like coils of rope were being twisted around my body tighter and tighter until I couldn't move. I had no one to talk to who knew anything about what happened. No one but Beth.

"How long have you been volunteering?"

"Six months," she answered, and I felt the invisible ropes squeeze again.

"What do you do regularly? Like when you're not volunteering."

"I'm in school to get my social work degree."

She was a student. Probably not that much older than me and Ani. I released a breath. Desperation plucked along my skin. I knew I should hang up. But the fear of being left utterly alone with Ani's problems was too much.

"Ani's messed up," I finally told her. Part of me knew it was worthless. She couldn't help. Probably wasn't even supposed to be talking to me.

"Well, that's not surprising, but what do you mean by messed up?" she answered calmly. "What's going on?" She had her official counselor voice on and I almost hung up again, but I couldn't stomach the idea of talking to a random, probably equally unqualified "volunteer" on the rape crisis hotline.

"She's messing around with other guys." I waited for Beth to respond, but she didn't say anything. Were all counselors like this? Did volunteer training include the art of nontalking? All the long pauses and awkward silences were annoying. "She tried to break up with me."

"And?" she prompted.

"I wouldn't let her. But she's messing around with other guys. I don't know what to do."

"It sounds like you're not comfortable with that," she said.

"Yeah, no shit. Of course I'm not comfortable with it. She's my girlfriend."

"Did you ask her why she was doing it?" Her voice was so mellow, I wanted to put my hand through the phone and squeeze her throat. Didn't she understand what I was saying?

"She said it was her choice what she wanted to do with her body," I answered through clenched teeth.

"And it is. But it sounds like there's more going on with

184

this. You know, promiscuity is a very common reaction in cases of rape."

"Again with the common reactions to rape? Is everything a common reaction to rape? If I told you she stopped bathing and wore the same clothes every day, would that be a common reaction?"

"Sometimes. Why? Is that happening?"

"No, but she *is* messing around with other guys."

"And that *is* a common reaction to rape," Beth said again.

"So?" I didn't feel better. I didn't give a shit if it was a common reaction. My girlfriend was hooking up with *other* guys.

She took a deep breath. "So sometimes blatant sexuality is a form of self-destructiveness. And sometimes girls and women get their identity wrapped up in the rape and don't see themselves as anything beyond a vessel for men's sexual needs."

"Oh, come on, Beth. A vessel for men's sexual needs? Give me a frickin' break."

Beth released a sigh. "Okay, let's just talk about Ani. Tell me, Ben, have you noticed a difference in her intimacy with you?"

"What do you mean?" I walked the length of my bedroom floor, scraping my feet along the carpet. Plush, ridiculous white carpet.

"Is she engaged? Is sex mutually beneficial? Is she looking to have her own needs met in the same way she had previously or is she focused on your needs exclusively?"

"In English, please."

"When you're together, do you make her feel good or does she make it all about you?"

Crap. Crap. My mind pulled at memories of the last few times we'd had sex. She seemed so into it at first, I hadn't really thought about it. But I hadn't gone down on her since the rape. She'd given me head a couple of times, but whenever I offered to reciprocate, she'd brushed me off. I figured she just wanted to get right to things. But after the last time, when she faked it, I didn't know how to read her.

"We haven't had sex in a while."

"Okay. Well, was that her decision?"

Fuck. "No. It's just that the last time, I realized she wasn't totally into it."

Silence.

"I—I didn't rape her," I stuttered. "It wasn't like that. I just got the feeling she wasn't really *with* me, you know?"

"So you haven't been trying to connect with her in that way?"

"No," I said at last, mentally cursing myself for being a selfish asshole. "She hasn't been engaged or whatever. She faked it the last time. Maybe the last few times. I don't know."

"Did you talk to her about it afterward?" she asked, and I winced at the sympathy in her voice. I didn't deserve it.

"Not really. I've tried to talk to her a bunch, but she doesn't want to get into it with me."

"Have you seen her with other guys? Or could it maybe just be rumors?"

I exhaled and stopped pacing my room to sit on my bed. "I heard it from a pretty reliable source."

"Listen, this is just my opinion, but I think when girls get angry, they turn it in on themselves. Guys tend to fight other people, girls feel bad about their emotions and punish themselves for it. Maybe that's what Ani is doing."

"What the hell is that supposed to mean?"

"Well." She released a sigh. "I don't know for sure since I haven't spoken to her, but I suspect Ani feels responsible in part for what happened. Whether it was from the drinking or possible date rape drugs, she feels like she put herself in the situation to be raped. So instead of dealing with these feelings of shame and doubt, she's becoming self-destructive. Doing something to numb the feelings. For her, it's sex. For some survivors, it's cutting or bulimia."

"This all sounds like it comes out of a 'very special episode' of some crappy TV show. Seriously. Are you reading from a book? This is Ani. She's not some poster girl for the damaging effects of irresponsible drinking or how rape can change your life. She's Ani. My Ani."

"Do you think she might talk to one of the counselors here?" she asked after several more seconds of silence passed. I wished she would. I was in way over my head.

"Probably not."

"I'll try calling her. Remind her that she can contact the hotline twenty-four hours a day. Have you decided what you want to do?"

I didn't know. I didn't know anything. I had hoped a conversation with Beth might help me figure things out, but now, I didn't even know if she knew what she was talking about. Or if she was just faking it like me. Saying what she was supposed to say because that's what they told her in some training.

I was confused and basically alone. Ani didn't deserve for me to bail on her, but how much was I going to have to take?

"Stick with her, I guess," I answered. "If she's with me, maybe she'll tone it all down, get back to herself. I'll try to do that stuff you said. Serve her needs or whatever." I never thought I'd be having this conversation. It was horrifying and humiliating all at once.

"Yes, if you decide to be intimate with her again, try to engage her," Beth said, clicking back into counselorspeak. "Make sure she sees herself as someone you want to be with as a whole person, not just this part of her."

Yeah, that'd be easy. Was I supposed to pull that off before or after she hooked up with the lacrosse team in the janitor's closet?

"Ben," Beth continued, "you know we have support groups for family and friends of survivors. We call it Healing Allies.

The times for the groups are on the organization's website if you're interested."

"Yeah, I don't know about that, but thanks anyway."

I hung up and went online to read more about rape trauma syndrome. There were so many different kinds of sexual assault and so many different reactions to it that my head wanted to explode. I found myself in one of those survivor forums online and got in a chat with a seventeen-year-old girl who'd been sexually abused by her babysitter for years. She told me the best thing to do for Ani was support her and encourage her to talk to someone.

I checked out times for Healing Allies but didn't think I could go. I imagined myself sitting with a bunch of parents and husbands of rape victims, and I couldn't see me saying anything or telling Ani's story.

The whole thing was stupid. I wasn't a support group guy. Most of the girls in the forums probably thought I was some stalker. Maybe they hadn't even been raped and were just on there for attention or because they were bored. Resentment made me worthless as a boyfriend, and I couldn't figure out enough to make any kind of definitive move beyond trying to do what Beth said.

I went over to Ani's after I got off the computer. I tried to talk to her without mentioning the lacrosse thing. I didn't think I'd be able to even look at her if she tried to explain it. I wasn't even sure I could get hard thinking about other guys' dicks in her. Which made me feel like an even bigger prick.

Ani wouldn't talk about anything anyway; she kept kissing my neck and moving my hands to her boobs.

"Ani, cut it out," I finally said.

"What?" She pouted. "I just want to be with you. It's been a long time since we've been alone together. Don't you want me anymore?"

I took a deep breath and remembered Beth's words. "Of course I do." I rubbed my hands over her shoulders. "When's your mom going to be home?"

She smiled, but it didn't quite make it to her whole face. "Late. She's preparing for her art class, getting supplies, and setting up the room. We have another two hours, at least."

"Okay, take your clothes off."

Her face didn't react. She just shoved her clothes onto the floor like she was getting changed for work or something. I tried not to cringe. She tugged at my shirt, but I pushed her away.

"Lie down."

She looked at me suspiciously.

"Please. Ani."

She kissed me and pulled me toward her, while positioning herself underneath me on the bed. There were too many blankets on it, but I didn't care. I didn't want to ruin things with questions about why her bed still looked like a fort.

I drew away and started to trace my hand slowly along her arms. I kissed her clavicle bone. She used to love when I dipped my tongue along the hollow skin and I'd always considered it one of the sexiest parts of her. She froze.

"Why aren't you taking off your clothes?" she asked, stilling my kisses.

I slid my hands to her legs and traced small patterns along her thigh. "I will. In a little bit. I want you to feel good first."

She shook her head and turned to her side.

"You need to be naked, Beez. And inside me. Now." Her voice had a little tremor. I hated the guys who did this to her, so much. Anger was burning a hole inside me. I wanted to scream. Instead, I tried to pour all my emotions back into her. Fill her up with something that wasn't pain and shit and other guys.

I rested my hand on her hip. "No. This is for you." I tried to move my hand between her legs, but her knees shot up to her chest.

"I don't want that."

"Ani," I begged, "please let me touch you."

I started to massage her neck and kissed her shoulder blades. She was curled up like a marble statue covered in skin. She wouldn't relax.

I moved my hand to her front and grazed my fingers across her chest. She'd always been one of those girls who liked me messing with her boobs, but instead of getting a response from her, I felt wetness.

I sat up. "Are you crying?"

Her hair hung over her face and she shook her head. I pushed a few strands back.

"Oh, Jesus, Ani. I just want to make you feel good. I don't want you to cry."

"Then stop," she whispered. "I don't want you to do this. This isn't about me."

I shot off the bed and ran my hands over my head. "Yes, Ani, it is. All of this is about you. What we do and what we don't do. It's been about you ever since the rape."

Ani sat up and grabbed her shirt. She pulled it over her head and wrapped herself in a blanket. "Fuck you, Ben. Don't throw that shit in my face. I've given you everything you wanted since then."

"Everything except my fucking girlfriend back. You think I just want your body. What the hell? How can you think that? After all the shit I've put up with?" I was pissed. I needed to keep my mouth shut, but I couldn't.

"Oh, poor Ben, you've had to deal with so much. It must be so taxing getting blow jobs. It's not easy dating the Manhole, is it?" She pounded on my chest. "Well, fuck you, I gave you an out. You wouldn't let me break up with you."

My hands shook. Ani was so screwed up. There was nothing I could do. I stalked to her closet and threw open the door. I found the bag of pamphlets from the hospital and pulled out the card with the crisis hotline number.

"Call them. You need help for this."

Ani turned her head into the pillow and screamed. I thought about the survivors online. They seemed so strong when they talked about what happened. So together.

I walked out the door like there was an eighty-pound weight on my shoulders. I got into my car and drove. I had no idea where I was going. I kept seeing Ani's tearful face asking me to stop touching her. Why did I feel like such a dick for trying to please my girlfriend?

The next day, I went to the rape crisis center for a Healing Allies meeting. Me. At a support group. This was what my life had come to. I didn't even have a lot of hope for it, but at least it felt like I was doing something. I walked into the brightly lit room and froze when I saw gray plastic chairs all in a circle. The carpet beneath my feet was the crappy industrial kind, worn and suspiciously barf-colored. I sat next to a chubby girl with frizzy curls who introduced herself as Sofia. She was taking classes at the community college and wanted to be a nurse. I mumbled my name and let her ramble on. When the overly tidy group "facilitator" walked in, I nearly bolted. Sofia's hand stopped me.

"Give him a chance," she whispered. "He looks like an idiot, but he's actually pretty good. And he's been through it."

I eyed the rest of the people in the room. As I suspected, there were several parents there, but there were also a couple of younger kids around Michael's age, and another guy with a pissed-off expression who was probably in the same boat as me.

"So, I'm Neil," the facilitator said, "and this is Healing Allies. Some of you have been here before but I see a few new faces." Neil directed his attention to me and the pissed-off dude. "Why don't you all go around and introduce yourselves and if you feel comfortable, explain why you're here?"

Oh, Christ. I'd stumbled into some sort of touchy-feely AA thing. I shifted in my seat and Sofia put her hand on my arm again. I shook it off. Who did this girl think she was?

Neil turned to Sofia. "Would you like to start, Sofia?"

She pushed her frizzy hair out of her face and took a deep breath. "Sure. I'm Sofia. I'm a sexual assault survivor as well as an ally. My brother sexually molested me for six years, and when I finally told my family, it came out that he had been molesting my cousin as well."

I gaped at her. I couldn't believe this girl just put herself out there like that. And she'd been molested by her brother for six years. Jesus. Six fricking years. My brain couldn't wrap itself around that. And the messed-up part was she didn't even seem that upset. I looked at the rest of the group to see if they were as shocked as I was. They all just looked normal. Except for the pissed-off dude, who was staring at his feet and ripping a hole in the bottom of his T-shirt. Sofia gave me an understanding smile.

"I've been in counseling for a really long time," she said in a low voice.

"Clearly," I muttered back. What the hell was I doing in this place? I didn't belong with these people.

Neil directed his attention to me. "Would you like to introduce yourself?"

I opened my mouth and took a breath. I looked at the faces staring back at me and shook my head. I couldn't do it. It felt like I was betraying Ani. I stood up and mumbled an apology. My cheeks flushed as I stumbled to the door and walked outside.

I leaned my head against the side of the building and took large breaths. Thirty seconds later Sofia exited.

"When did it happen?" She moved to the space next to me and sat cross-legged on the ground.

I slumped down next to her, careful not to get too close. "A couple months ago."

"Your girlfriend?" she asked.

I nodded.

"No one's gonna judge you in there. They're all going through the same thing."

I didn't answer.

"The first time I came to a meeting, I was with my parents. My mom cried almost the whole time, saying how it was her fault. It was horrible. I never wanted to come back."

I looked at her. Her face had tons of freckles on it and she'd obviously had acne problems when she was younger because she had some scarring.

"Why did you come back?"

"Because afterward, I went to see my cousin and she was a wreck. She was really angry with me. She told me if I had just said something in the first place, maybe she wouldn't have been raped by my brother."

The reality of her situation snapped at me again.

"Jesus Christ. Your own fricking brother? And he did it to your cousin, too?"

"Yeah. And if I'd said something, he probably wouldn't have gotten to her."

What was I supposed to say? I'd played the "if only" game enough to know where Sofia's cousin was coming from.

"At first I thought my cousin was right to blame me. I mean, she sort of *was* right, but this group helped me realize that I wasn't the one who assaulted her. It was my brother."

"Huh. Well, it seems like it worked out for you."

She laughed. "Yeah. Whatever that means."

I closed my eyes and thought of all the things Ani had said to me. All the things about it being her fault and only being good at one thing now. She didn't know how to go back. She couldn't let go of what happened and I didn't think I could walk away from her until she did. Part of me got that we couldn't be salvaged, but maybe Ani could. If Sofia could be raped by her brother and still show up at a crap support group every week, Ani might be able to get past things one day.

"Yeah. Whatever that means," I repeated.

"I was one of those girls who thought rape was a guy pulling you into an alley and holding a knife to your throat. I didn't think my own brother could do that to me. And I didn't want to tell anyone because it was my family."

"How come you did?"

"Because I didn't want it to keep happening anymore. I wanted to die, it was tearing me apart so much."

"So what happened?" I didn't even want to think about my sick fascination with this girl's story and how she actually seemed pretty fine after all the crap that happened to her.

"When I finally did say something, no one wanted to really talk about it. They all kind of freaked. Especially my mom. But then we all went to see someone. And my brother left for a while."

"Left where?"

She shrugged. "He did this sex offenders' treatment program. And he was old enough to move out, so he did."

"Do you still see him?"

"No. Not really."

"That's messed up." It was, but still, she was sitting here, not boning other guys; she was doing something about her shitty situation.

"And when I tell people about it now, they all look at me like I did something wrong. Like I should've said something sooner. Like it couldn't ever happen to them because they would be smarter than me."

I dropped my face into my hands. Was that why Ani didn't want to tell anyone the truth? Was she worried people would blame her? That they would say it was her fault?

"Do you want to talk about it?" Sofia asked.

I nodded but refused to look at her. I picked up a handful of tiny pebbles next to me and tossed one. I stared straight ahead and poured out the entire story of what'd happened, tossing pebbles throughout. At the end Sofia didn't say anything. She just gave me an awkward sisterly hug and handed me a slip of paper with her cell number on it if I ever wanted to talk.

"You should talk to a counselor, Ben," she said on her way back inside. "They can help. At the very least, come back to group. You'd be amazed. You're not the only one going through something like this."

She waved to me, and a small knot inside my stomach uncurled. I'd told my story. Ani's story. I had no answers, but somehow, it seemed easier having put it out in the world, even if it was to a strange girl who had enough problems of her own.

23

I drove around for over an hour after I left Sofia. Past school, past my house, past the zoo. I parked on the street behind Ani's place and sat. The temperature had dropped and I shivered in my car, unable to get out and go talk to Ani. My phone pinged. Text from Kevin.

Coach said if you miss another practice, he's pulling you from the relay team.

I was supposed to be in the pool three hours a day during winter break. To get my times back and, as Coach put it, pull my head out of my ass. I'd be lucky if I got in the pool once. Coach *should* drop me from the relay team. My times sucked anyway. I was dead weight to Kevin and the other guys. The frickin' fish out of water. I didn't bother texting Kevin back.

Sofia's words zipped around my head, but none of them

stuck. They all started to feel like bullshit in the same way that Beth's did. Like that's what you say to the family and friends of rape victims because everyone is too afraid to tell you the truth. That it doesn't fucking get better. That you spin your wheels and it just gets worse.

When I got too cold to sit any longer, I walked to Ani's. She swung the door open like she was expecting me, but only as a burden she couldn't let go of. I didn't tell her anything about Healing Allies. I asked her if she was okay, if she wanted to talk about the sex thing, but she shook her head and led me into the kitchen where she made us quesadillas. We ate in silence and I racked my brain for a topic of conversation that wouldn't cause any more damage to the two of us.

Gayle walked in while we were still eating.

"Ben, it's so nice to see you. It's been too long," she said, and squeezed my shoulder.

"Yeah. Uh, how's your class going?" I asked as she tore off a piece of Ani's quesadilla and popped it in her mouth. She smoothed Ani's hair but didn't see her flinch. God, how could she not see what was happening to her own daughter?

"Good. It's actually just a short camp to keep kids entertained and out of their parents' hair while they're on vacation. What are you up to this winter break? Is your family staying in town?"

"Yeah, my mom's having some of her relatives over for

Christmas Eve, but then we'll probably just hang out and play board games on Christmas Day. It's sort of a family ritual," I answered, tracking Ani's facial expression. It remained completely blank.

"Oh, that sounds nice. Maybe we should do something like that, Ani?" She rubbed Ani's back and must have noticed her sudden tensing because she quirked her head slightly.

"Maybe," Ani replied, and took a bite of quesadilla.

Gayle's eyes met mine in question and when I didn't respond, she refocused on Ani. Awkward silence pressed against the three of us. I desperately wanted Gayle to ask something that might open Ani up, but she just kept looking between the two of us. Ani chewed her food slowly while she spun the plate in front of her. I kept waiting for it to slip off the island. Crack into a bunch of pieces on the ground so that maybe we could say something about broken things.

"It'd be nice to get to spend time just the two of us," Gayle finally said with her eyes trained on Ani's face. "You've been out so much lately. It'll be good to have some mother-daughter bonding time." She turned toward me and gave me a fake, bright smile. "And you need to stop planning so many evening outings with my daughter. She can be home sometimes too, not just always at your house."

I swallowed a lump of quesadilla and glanced at Ani. We hadn't been to my house in almost a month. Where had Ani been going all these nights? And who was she going out with? I took a sip of the lemonade Ani had poured me and tried not to puke up everything I'd just eaten.

Ani's empty eyes met mine and she offered me a tiny shake of her head.

I looked back to Gayle. "Okay. Sure. We can hang out here, too."

Gayle nodded, grabbed one more bite of Ani's food, and walked out the kitchen door, mumbling about moody kids.

I wouldn't have sex with Ani that night. Even after Gayle left and Ani climbed into my lap. I wouldn't let her touch me the next night either. I told her I couldn't be with her until we talked about what happened. She refused. It tore me up to turn her down because I could see how much my rejection stung. But I also realized that sex was somehow pushing us further apart and I wasn't interested in being one of *those guys* anymore.

The problem was that Ani got more and more sullen. I'd bring over movies to watch, and she'd stare out the window the entire time they were on. I'd try to hold her hand, and she'd pull away. She wouldn't talk to me, she wouldn't talk to Kate, she wouldn't talk to Beth when she called. She was completely shutting down, and I didn't know what I could do about it.

I drove to the pool every day but somehow couldn't find it

in me to get out of my Jeep and practice. So I sat and stewed, trying to figure out what might break through Ani's shell. None of my ideas seemed to be working. Desperation started to creep over me. I knew it was happening, could feel it every morning as I woke up more shredded than the day before. Hours spent with Ani left me hollow and alone. I needed to get out, but every time I thought about leaving, I remembered the way she curled into my lap in the front hallway of school and cried her eyes out.

And I remembered how she used to be and thought maybe I just needed to try harder, find something that would actually work. Kevin texted me, but I couldn't do more than send clipped responses back. I was fine. Everything was fine. I wasn't feeling good. Too sick to make it to swim practice. Bullshit excuse after bullshit excuse.

The loneliness started to eat away at me, and out of hopelessness, I went back online to a survivors' forum. The rape stories may have been made up, but they were closer to real than anything I had with Ani. I talked about Ani and what was happening with us. The other survivors told me to keep trying, not to push Ani, but to be present for her. Their words soothed me in a way I hadn't felt since I took Ani home from the hospital. But still, a part of me understood that it was all smoke and mirrors. Their stories weren't Ani's. My reality was my own.

I spent too much time on the computer. My mom popped

her head in more than once and said she was concerned I was becoming addicted to cyber porn. She was joking, but her eyes looked past me at the blank screen with my chat window up. Cyber porn might have been easier. Instead, I was addicted to fixing Ani.

When I was at Ani's, I acted like we were okay and tried to ignore the cracking pieces of us. When I was home, I stayed online, waiting, hoping, pretending it wasn't that big a deal to crave solace from strangers.

GuerGirl24: Everyone told me I needed to get over it. But it took me so long because I never felt completely safe. It was like I was always on my guard. I still am. Give Ani time; she's hurting more than you know.

"Ani," I said one afternoon when we were sitting on her couch.

"Yeah?"

"Do you want to go check out the Zoo Lights? They're supposed to be pretty cool. My mom told me they give you hot chocolate and sing carols on the Motor Safari tour." I was grasping at straws, but I couldn't stand being in Ani's apartment any longer.

"I don't think so, Bumble."

"Why not? It'll be fun. Remember? The zoo's kind of our place."

Ani stared at me for a long time. Finally she said, "The zoo's not our place. We don't have a place anymore. We have an apartment that you visit, but it's just a holding space. A cage for the two of us to walk around in, staring at each other, wondering who's going to get out first." She stood up and got my coat from the closet without saying another word.

As I drove home, all I could think was: How much time would I have to give her?

Niki4347: I didn't remember anything after my rape. I didn't tell anyone for a long time because I didn't want to remember. I just wanted to survive.

"I'm not up for chatting today, Ben," Ani said before I had walked two feet into her room. "You need to either sleep with me or head back home."

I stared at the ceiling and counted to ten. "I'm not sleeping with you until we talk about what happened."

"Jesus, why can't I be with someone who wants me?" Her eyes filled with tears, and I felt like such a dick, I nearly gave in.

"You know I want you. Don't turn this around on me. But I won't have you that way."

Ani pointed to the door. "Then leave. Now. I'm not up for you today."

When I got home, I asked one of the online survivors how she was able to move past the rape. I didn't want to pry, but I was running out of ideas to help Ani. The survivor told me her parents believed her and she got counseling and it was enough. I rubbed my eyes and stared at the picture of Ani tacked on my bulletin board. Why wasn't I enough for her? I had buried my doubts about what happened at the party so deep, she didn't even know they existed, and still I wasn't enough. It killed me.

TaylrGrl99: I didn't think I could come back from it. For a long time, I didn't even want to. But people cared and I faced it and made myself whole again.

"I didn't mean to hurt your feelings the other day," Ani said when I brought her a peppermint mocha and a teddy bear with a ribbon around its neck the day after Christmas.

"I know."

"I made you something," she said, and smiled shyly. Warmth moved through me. "I've been working on it awhile. I thought it might help you keep warm in the winter."

She pulled out a lopsided black-and-yellow striped hat. I grinned.

"I knitted it. See, it's bee colors, you know?"

"Yeah, I got that." I pulled it on my head. It was at least five sizes too big, but it was the most perfect thing I'd ever gotten from Ani. "It's awesome. Thanks."

I leaned in to kiss her and she kissed me back softly. I moved a bit closer and nearly sobbed the minute I felt her change, open up her mouth and shut down her emotions. I pulled back, but she hung on to me and ground herself into my leg.

"Ani, stop. Don't make this into that. I kissed you because I love the hat. I love that you made something. You haven't done that in forever. No necklaces or painting or anything. This is a really big deal. I don't want anything else from you."

Her huge eyes filled with tears. I tried to hug her but she stepped away from me.

"I'm sorry," she said, her voice shaking. "That's all I have for you right now, Beez. That's all I have to give."

I left Ani's house that night wearing the hat. She didn't say anything about it. I'd damaged her by stopping sex this time and I didn't know how to undo it.

Kevin was waiting for me when I got home.

"You don't look sick," he said as soon as I walked into my living room.

I shrugged and glanced around. My parents and Michael were playing Uno in the kitchen. Dad's Haitian music chimed from the speakers. "I can't swim."

"You can swim. You're *not* swimming, but you *can* swim. Jesus Christ, it's enough, dude. You've had enough. You're my friend so I'm telling you this for your own good. Get out of this. Now."

"You have no idea what you're talking about."

"The fuck I don't. That girl's a mess and she's pulled you into her vortex of doom, and if someone doesn't drag you out, the two of you are gonna drown."

"Oh, Jesus, stop being so dramatic." I whipped my hat off and tucked it into my coat pocket.

"I'm not being dramatic. I'm being realistic. Do you even love this girl anymore?"

His question hit me in the chest. Christ. Did I? "I don't know. It doesn't seem like it matters that much. I think I can help her, get her back."

"Dude, that's bullshit bravado. And I gotta be honest, at this point, all I'm worried about is getting you back."

I stood up and crossed to the front door. "I'm not fucking lost. She is. She needs me. She needs someone to believe her and help her."

Kevin pulled on his jacket and followed me to the door. "Dude, you have no idea what you've gotten yourself into. This isn't fixable. How many more times am I gonna have to have this conversation with you?"

"None. I don't want to discuss it with you anymore. My girlfriend. My business."

Kevin barked out a hollow laugh. "Yeah. Your *girlfriend*. I think there might be a few guys who'd disagree with you on that."

I pulled my arm back to hit him, but he ducked and darted from the door. "Go to hell!" I shouted after him.

"I'm already there, bro. Visiting you and Ani, the girl you aren't even sure you love."

When I got to my room, I texted Sofia from Healing Allies and told her what happened. I'd been thinking about her a lot since telling her my story the night of group. I hadn't gone back and wouldn't, but I was frantic to find someone who understood what I was going through. Someone who would tell me I was doing the right thing. She texted back and asked me if I could be with Ani still, even if she wasn't ever completely whole again. I couldn't answer truthfully. I felt too guilty and knew I was a complete shit for thinking, *I don't think so.*

24

After break, when we got back to school, Ani turned into a complete ghost. She started missing classes. She avoided all of us. She stopped eating with us, stopped showing up at lunch most days. I saw her in the hall with different guys and tried to pretend I didn't notice. I was paralyzed as to what to do. When I'd finally screw up my courage to break things off with her, she'd do something like take my hand in the hall and tell me she was excited to go to my next swim meet. For every flash I got of the old Ani, there would be hours of the new Ani, cold indifference plastered on her face. But the flashes still existed and I still hoped.

I went to swim practice and couldn't get my shit together in the pool. Coach told me he was going to recommend some- one else for my scholarship. I should have felt bad, but too many other things had taken over that space in my body. A lost scholarship seemed like nothing.

My mom started asking me questions at home. I had no answers. Our family dinners were filled with everyone staring at me while I pretended everything was fine.

"I've decided we should go back to Haiti for your spring vacation," my dad announced one night.

I pushed the rice around on my plate and kept my eyes down.

"Your father and I think we all need to reconnect," Mom said, watching me spear a green bean.

Michael looked at me. I didn't say anything. "It'd be a good idea, Ben. Don't you think?"

I swallowed a tasteless lump of food. "Sure. It's been a while since we've seen Grandpa," I said to my dad.

He scrutinized me. I kept my face blank, not letting my dad's keen perception tear down the house of cards I'd so carefully built with my family.

"And I think we could all use a break from things," he said with a nod.

I shrugged. I wanted to go to Haiti. I felt different when I was there, part of something bigger. But the thought of Ani on her own for ten days paralyzed me. What would happen to her? Would she even miss me?

My mom got up to get a glass of water. She touched my

212

hand when she returned to the table. "It'll give us a chance to talk."

I stuffed the rest of my roll in my mouth and chewed slowly, unwilling to offer my family anything else. I didn't have it in me to say anything to them. I was too tired to face the consequences of their help.

My mom turned to Michael and dabbed a piece of food off his face with her napkin. He batted her hand away.

"Cut it out, Mom," he said. "I'm not four."

I elbowed him and nodded. He grinned at me and rolled his eyes at Mom. Relief tugged at my stomach. The two of us were okay as brothers. At least I had that.

I sat through dinner until I couldn't stand it anymore, then bolted from the table and retreated to my room.

I continued to go online to rape forums almost every night, asking advice from strangers on what to do. It was stupid. But it was all I had. Everyone seemed to say the same thing: *Be there when she's ready to talk.* Then ignoring my growing guilt, I texted Sofia. We spent less time talking about Ani and formed sort of a strange friendship. Neither of us mentioned what I figured we both knew—I was betraying Ani by turning to Sofia. I was too exhausted to care. Sofia was like a secret-keeping sister to me and I had no interest in giving her up.

I still tried to find Ani in between classes. Sometimes she was with other guys. Mostly she was alone. Just like I'd left her at that party. I reminded her I would support her any way she needed me to. She looked through me and almost never responded.

I found her in the art room one day after school and the relief nearly buckled me.

"You're painting," I said, walking up behind her.

She jumped a little but turned to me with a smile. "Yeah. I had this dream last night. Crazy. I wanted to paint it."

"It's been a long time since you've been in here."

She nodded. I stared past her and blinked at the painting. Harsh blues and blacks swirled around a naked girl. Naked Ani. Slashes of red on the insides of her thighs. I looked closer. Not swirls of blue and black, but dark, horned monsters. Scribbly writing covered the bottom of the picture. I leaned forward, trying to make out the words. *At night she was haunted by demons and monsters and the boy who liked to play with fire.*

"Jesus," I whispered.

"It's not finished yet. I still haven't added the boy with the lighter."

"Ani," I said, and shut my eyes. "I'm sorry. I should've been there."

What the hell else could I say? I should ask about the dream, but I couldn't. I knew what it was about. Part of me was glad she'd painted it. I hoped it would make things better, make her not have bad dreams. Maybe it could be an outlet for her. But as soon as I thought it, I saw the shutters close over her eyes again.

She picked up a large can of black paint and poured it over the top of the painting.

"What are you doing?"

She covered the painted mess with a cloth and grabbed her bag. "Nothing. It was stupid anyway. Let's go."

When I was at school and didn't have the computer or Sofia, I talked to Kate. Ani had blown her off too.

"The thing that bugs me the most," Kate said one day at lunch, "is that this totally isn't her. Ani's not a sneak-around-and-be-evasive kind of person. She's called me on my shit from day one. You too. I just don't get why she won't let us help her."

"Maybe she blames you?" Kevin asked.

Kate turned her death stare on him.

He held up his hands. "I'm not saying it's fair or anything, I'm just saying that a part of her may blame the two of you for not keeping her safe at the party."

Kate's eyes brimmed with tears. I handed her a napkin.

"It wasn't your fault," I said. "There wasn't much you could do. It would've been different if I was there. But Ani made her own choices at that party. And so did the bastards who messed with her."

Kate brushed away tears. "I could've done something. I saw it happening. I was just so angry about what she said to me. She was being such a bitch. I should have seen she was in over her head."

I patted her hand and hoped she would stop crying. I couldn't take much more of girls crying. And I couldn't think about the events of the party anymore. Ani's ass in some guy's hands. Ani table dancing. Ani making out with someone else. The reality of her at the party and the reality of her since the rape were too close for me to think about.

Ani walked up to our table and looked at Kate's hand in mine. "Are you fucking Kate?"

I reeled back. "Of course not. What are you talking about?"

She shrugged. "Maybe she'll have more luck with you than I have."

Her words were like darts piercing my skin. Accusation and defeat seeped into the space between us.

"Why are you being such a bitch, Ani?" Kate asked.

"It doesn't matter," Ani responded, and started to walk away. I grabbed her hand and she turned back to me.

"I'm not hooking up with Kate. I'm with you," I said firmly.

Ani laughed and it nearly swallowed me. "No, *you* are definitely not with me. But trust me, you're among the minority. Just ask your friend Kevin." She winked at him and walked away.

I swiveled in my seat and stared at Kevin. "Don't even tell me you've messed around with Ani."

He shifted in his seat. "No, man, of course not." Red splotches popped up on his neck.

"Then what is she talking about?" I asked, clenching my jaw. Dammit. I could barely breathe. It was a constant shit spiral and I needed to get out.

"I don't know," he said, his gaze avoiding mine.

"Kevin. What the hell happened?"

"Nothing. I didn't do anything with her. I swear," he said.

"Then what?" I looked at him and waited.

Kevin squeezed the muscles on his neck and finally met my stare. "I walked in on her going down on some guy in the locker room during gym class."

I gaped at him. "When?" I asked as calmly as I could.

"Last week."

"How'd she know you were there?" Every part of my body shook. I was so disgusted with Ani. So disgusted with myself.

Kevin took a deep breath. "She saw me. The guy didn't because he had his eyes closed, but she saw me. She signaled me to come closer. I took off. She texted me afterward to ask if I liked the show. It was totally messed up. I didn't even answer her text."

I crumbled my lunch into a ball and tossed it in the trash

can. I grabbed my coat and Ani's bee hat from my locker. I walked out the school doors, got in my car, and drove. I didn't want to go home. I wished I could leave town. I needed to get away. I turned the radio up and pulled to the side of the road and cried. I hadn't cried hard tears since my dog died when I was nine years old, but I was wrung out. I felt as hollow as Ani looked.

25

I finally wiped my face and called Sofia. Our weird relationship had always been about texting; I'd never called her before. She'd never even suggested it. It always seemed like it crossed a line that I wasn't quite ready to go over.

She picked up on the first ring. Her voice sounded younger than I remembered and so different from the cracked emptiness of Ani.

"It's Ben. Can you talk?" My voice sounded hoarse. I cleared my throat.

"Yeah, I don't have class until tonight. What's up? Is Ani okay?"

"She thinks I'm messing around with one of her friends." I heard Sofia's little gasp. "And she doesn't even seem to care,"

I blurted out. I shut my eyes to the raw memory of Ani's indifferent accusation.

"Oh, Ben, I'm so sorry. Did she say she doesn't care?"

"Not in so many words, but I got the general idea. It wasn't the worst part, though."

Sofia stayed silent on the other end. I had to check my phone to see if we were still connected.

"My friend Kevin saw her going down on some guy in gym class. And then she pretty much offered herself up to Kevin afterward. It was disgusting."

"God, things are really bad with her right now. What did you do?"

A weird grumble came from my throat. "What do you think I did? I took off. I couldn't stand to look at her or Kevin. I mean, how long do I have to watch this mess?"

"Ben," Sofia said softly. "I'm glad you called. Don't get me wrong. I want to help you. But why are you asking me this? Why are you on the phone with *me*?"

"Because," I answered, trying not to cry again, "I don't know who else to talk to."

"Ani," she said. "Go talk to Ani. About all of this. Don't avoid anything. Be honest and see if you guys can start from there."

"I'm not sure I can," I said, and this time, I did choke on tears.

"Then tell her that. Tell her it's tearing you apart and she needs to get help. Don't give her an ultimatum, but tell her how you feel. It's the only thing you can do for her now."

I clicked off with Sofia, and doubt rested in my gut. It'd been going on too long with too much shit piled up. But Ani deserved the conversation, even if she didn't want it. I was determined to have it out with her one way or another. I couldn't stand by and watch everything fall apart any longer. Nothing I had done had worked.

I planned on taking Ani home and not letting her go until she agreed to talk to someone about everything. A rape counselor, her mom, the people on the hotline, I didn't care as long as she did something. There was a good chance I'd lose her after my intervention, but I had nothing left of my Ani, so it didn't seem like that big a risk.

Kevin had seen her going down on another guy. Jesus. *You're definitely not with me*. Ani's venomous words scraped over me. I wasn't. I wasn't with her. I was part of her problem as far as I could tell.

I drove back to school in time for the final bell. I pushed through swarms of kids trying to get out for the day. I scanned the halls looking for Ani but couldn't find her. I texted Kevin and Kate to ask if they'd seen her. *She's meeting with Mr. Pinter*, Kate texted back, and I ignored the tightening in my stomach.

221

Instead, I practiced the words I would say to her in my head. If I wasn't *with* her, then I could at least lay everything bare. Force her to get the help she needed.

I hated that she was meeting with Mr. Pinter. Old, fat Mr. Pinter, who spent most of his days lecturing to girls' chests. I'd heard sick rumors about him but never believed them. Why was Ani meeting him?

I raced to his classroom, but his door was closed and locked. I heard voices inside and pressed my ear to the door, hoping no one would notice the crazy eavesdropper in the hall. Mr. Pinter's low mumble was followed by Ani's phony, tittering laugh.

I banged on the door. No one answered, but the room suddenly got quiet. I banged on the door again. Nothing. What the fuck?

My entire body started to sweat. I tore down the hall and out the exit. A half a dozen people called to me outside, but I ignored them all. I circled the building and ducked into the evergreen bushes alongside the windows of Mr. Pinter's room. My heart thudded as I peered up into the first window. The shades were drawn. I inched farther down the outer wall and checked the second window. The shades were drawn there, too.

Jesus. What was I doing? What the hell had become of me? My system was on autopilot. Determination and desperation mashed together in my gut. It was like the final lap of a relay and I was way behind, pulling out everything that I had.

I stepped back from the wall and eyed the entire bank of windows. All of them had the shades drawn fully except for the last. About six inches of open window were left at the bottom. He must have left it open after third period, when the school always got overly hot.

I sucked in a deep breath and made my way down to it. I sat beneath the window on the frozen ground and listened. A deep moan sounded from within and I closed my eyes and counted. Finally I stood up and stared into Mr. Pinter's classroom.

He sat at his desk chair with his pants pushed to his ankles, and Ani crouched between his legs. Her hands gripped his thighs, and he tugged on her head, pushing her deeper into his lap. She had on her winter coat still, part of it trapped underneath the wheel of his chair.

"That's it. Take it all," he moaned, and my hands shook.

It made me sick to watch, but I couldn't turn away. I willed Ani to see me and suddenly she turned her head in my direction. At the same time, Mr. Pinter barked out a loud curse and grasped her ponytail tightly. Her wide, empty eyes watched me as he held her in place and pulsed into her mouth. Finally he sat back, pulled his pants up, and patted her on the shoulder.

She stood up without breaking eye contact with me. She yanked at the coat and it tore at the bottom. She slowly wiped her mouth and waited to see what I would do. I snatched the knitted bee hat from my head and threw it on the ground. Her hands brushed away the dust on her knees. When I didn't stop staring, she turned away, picked up her backpack, slid her hand along Mr. Pinter's zipper without even looking at him, and walked out the door.

I barfed on the frozen ground until there was nothing left inside of me. I was still dry heaving when Ani walked up, leaned over me, and picked up the hat.

"You've wrecked us. Wrecked me," I choked out.

She played with a loose piece of yarn on the rim. "I know."

I wiped my mouth and crawled into a seated position. She dropped next to me.

"Do you even care?"

She handed me the hat. "Yes."

"Then why are you doing this? All of it?"

Her fingers found the rip in her coat. "You have no idea what my life is like now, Bumble. I told you, this is who I am."

The bile still burned the back of my throat. "Fuck that. Enough with that. You made this choice."

She stood up and brushed the ice flakes from her coat. "You don't move on from something like that party."

"Yes, people can. They have. It's not—"

"All that stuff about healing. It's crap. You might forget sometimes. You might pretend you're fine. But then one day, you're outside and someone totally innocently asks to borrow a lighter. Or you see a girl drinking too much and you wonder if she'll get home that night. It stays with you forever."

She took a step away from me and my insides tore open.

"Why?" I shouted. "Why would you do that? With him? That sicko pervert?" I pointed to Mr. Pinter's window. "It's disgusting. How could you even consider it?"

She blinked her eyes at me once. Twice. "Don't you see? If I don't hate myself, I don't feel anything at all. At least disgust feels better than nothing."

She shuffled away, barely lifting her boots as she walked, not looking back. It was too much. I could never understand it. Not how she explained it. I sort of hated myself for even thinking I could help in the first place. What the hell did I know? I was basically just a kid with a messed-up girlfriend. Deluded into thinking I could do something to fix her.

Snow started to fall as I sat unmoving on the ground. I didn't feel the cold, didn't feel anything but numbness and the absolute certainty that everything I'd done over the past few months hadn't meant anything. Pieces of me and Ani were strewn all over, and there was no regluing us. Even the anger started to seep out of me. It took too much energy to maintain. I didn't fucking care anymore and that was the worst part of all of it. Kevin was right. Somehow, I'd gotten just as lost as Ani. Clinging to bullshit hopes fueled by people I didn't even really know. When the truth was, at the end of it all, there was just me and Ani. In a cage. Waiting to see who would leave first.

My hands trembled as I pulled my cell out of my back pocket. Tears rolled down my face and landed on my hand, each cool drop slicing through another layer of me. I shut my eyes for a few seconds, released a deep breath, and called Gayle. The phone rang and Ani disappeared farther down the block. I was done. Undone. Ani wasn't mine to patch up any longer. But even as Gayle's voice cut through the line and I opened my mouth to speak, I wasn't sure if I had escaped the cage or if Ani had.

Resources

The Voices and Faces Project
www.voicesandfaces.org

RAINN (Rape, Abuse & Incest National Network)
www.rainn.org
1-800-656-HOPE

Victim Rights Law Center
www.victimrights.org

CounterQuo
www.counterquo.org

Men Can Stop Rape
www.mencanstoprape.org

Rape Treatment Center
www.911rape.org

Rape Victim Advocates
www.rapevictimadvocates.org